Through the

Storms

and the *Rain*

Other Books by Francine A. Yates

Carrie O and Me: What A Woman God Made

Linda Smith returns to her old neighborhood. Her emotions are mixed with haunting childhood memories and the appreciation for the God-fearing family that adopted her. She flashes back to the times of being cared for by a woman who devoted her life to God and goodness. Linda is also on a mission to fulfill a promise she made on the deathbed of Mrs. Carrie O. That promise was to make peace with her birth mother Vivian, and forgive her for the pain she inflicted upon her in childhood. Linda's story is one of triumph over adversities and hope over despair. Her deep abiding faith provides the foundation of her success. Be prepared not to put this book down until the very end.

Faith Holds the Key (sequel)

Linda is trying to hold onto her belief, that her faith holds the key. But that faith is tested on this life's journey when she has to untangle a web of deceit. Wanting to look forward to a wonderful and promising future with the man she loves, Linda finds that she is pulled back into the past. Is her faith in God enough to give her the strength she needs?

This book is a work of fiction. All events, characters, places and incidents are strictly products of the author's imagination. Any resemblances in this book to actual persons, living or dead are completely coincidental.

Scripture quotations are taken from the King James Version of the Bible.

ISBN: 978-0-9778521-3-0 (paperback)

Published by Yates Publishing, LLC
P.O. Box 18982
Indianapolis, IN 46218

Printed in the United States of America

Through the
Storms
and the
Rain

Francine A. Yates

For we wrestle not against flesh and blood, but against principalities, against powers, against the rulers of the darkness of this world, against spiritual wickedness in high places. Wherefore take unto you the whole armour of God, that ye may be able to withstand in the evil day, and having done all, to stand.

Ephesians 6:12-13

Dedication

I would like to dedicate this book to my beloved husband, Benjamin F. Yates, who passed away August 15, 2009. May God keep you in His hands until we meet again!

To my family, who have taught me so much about life and how to love people everywhere, I thank you!!

Also to my prayer partner, Ms. Josephine Charleston, who has prayed for me from the beginning of my writing career until now, please continue to keep me lifted up in prayer.

Pastor James R. & Connie Pruitt
Pleasant Union Missionary Baptist Church

Acknowledgments

First and foremost, to God be the glory for the many things He has done to bless my life and writing career.

Also, I would like to acknowledge some of the most wonderful Christian women who have supported me through words and deeds and for that I will always be grateful. Etoria Wilson, Bettie Turner, Peggy Fishback, Margie Shivers, Cheryl Shockley, and Joanne Alexovich.

Last, but not least, to all the book clubs throughout the country and bookstores that have supported me, I thank you for adding *Through the Storms and the Rain* to your book collections. And of course, to all my readers everywhere, thank you for supporting me!

Chapter One

As I sit here holding and rocking my three- week- old daughter, Brianna. I feel the tears of joy welling in my eyes. I'm so thankful to God for this precious little bundle of joy. I'm also prayerful that Brandon and I can be the kind of parents Mrs. Carrie and Mr. Mack were to me. I want to teach Brianna the words of God and most of all I want her to live a God-fearing life.

As I lay Brianna down in the crib and cover her in the soft pink blanket Mom and Dad gave us, I hear the opening of the side door. It's Brandon coming home from being at the hospital most of the night.

Whispering, he said "Hey, why are you in the nursery?"

Turning to answer him I noticed he looks as if the door frame is holding him up. I could tell he was very, very tired. I said, "I knew you would be coming home soon and I didn't want the baby to cry and disturb you."

"I'm so tired that when I hit those sheets, I won't hear anything. We had to deliver two babies and a set of twins. The twins were early and had to be taken by C- section."

"Since Brianna is sleeping, why don't you take a seat in this rocking chair and I'll go and make you some breakfast."

Rubbing his eyes and yawning at the same time, Brandon said, "Linda, you do know what time it is, don't you?"

"No. I just know that Brianna is on a two hour feeding schedule. When she starts crying I get up and breast feed her."

"It's 4:00 in the morning. All I want is a hot shower and some sleep. The other two doctors are on call tomorrow so I can sleep most of the morning."

"Brandon, please don't sleep too long. You haven't forgotten that your sister and Carlos are here have you? They arrived just before dark. "

"No. I did notice their rental car out front. Lynda also called before they boarded the plane. All she talked about was how much Carlos Jr. has grown and about all the gifts she had in her suitcase for the baby."

"I can't wait for you to see little Carlos. He looks just like his father and he crawls everywhere. Go on and get some sleep so you can visit with them later. They will only be here for the next three days.

You really did use your head by partnering with the three other doctors. Now, they're on- call and you're free to spend the next few days with Lynda and Carlos."

Brandon leaned over, lightly kissed me on the lips and Brianna on her soft rosy cheeks. Then, stretching and yawning, he said, "I'm off to the showers and bed."

As he left the room I looked down at our little precious angel; looking just like Brandon and sleeping so peacefully. I don't want to disturb her, but I'm still tired and I don't want to sleep in this rocking chair-not when there's another unoccupied bedroom. I reached down to cuddle her in my arms and held her close as we walked down the hall to the spare bedroom for a few more hours of sleep.

Like clock work, I heard a cry and looked over on the nightstand—it was 6:30. Brianna was moving, kicking, and crying. She wanted to be fed again. I put her pacifier in her mouth so there would be no noise while I changed her diaper. I was able to fool her a little while but she started whining and kicking again. I got comfortable, held her in my arms and nursed her until she fell back to sleep. I laid her on her right side, put some pillows around her and made my way to the bathroom for a quick shower before anyone woke up.

After my shower and while dressing all I could think about was a piece of bacon and scrambled egg. I took one last look to make sure Brianna was still sleeping. I almost made it to the kitchen when the phone started ringing. I rushed to answer it before it disturbed everyone in the house who still had the pleasure of sleeping.

"Hello."

"Hi Linda, it's Mom. I know you're probably tired and remembered you said Lynda and her family was visiting, so I'm willing to take some pressure off of you, come over and cook breakfast for them."

"Thanks. What a great idea! I can use your help. Brandon spent most of the night at the hospital so he's still asleep. If I'm in the family room nursing the baby, come in the side door. I'll leave it open."

"I'll be there in about a half-an- hour. Do you want me to bring anything for breakfast?"

"I have everything but orange juice."

"Okay, I'll stop and bring some. Bye."

What a difference 14 months can make. I remember

when I was about to marry   Brandon. My mother and I weren't on good terms and I didn't even know if she was going to be at my wedding. My father was there to support me, though and just as I was about to finish getting dressed, mom came in apologizing and crying. We hugged and cried together.

Later my dad came looking for me. He walked in; it was like magic when Mom and Dad looked into each other eyes. They hadn't seen each other since my mother was pregnant with me and run out of town by her parents. My father's eyes got big as golf balls. He rushed towards her and said, "Vivian, is that you?" My mother said, "Yes, Alphonso, it's me." I will never forget that special moment. Here I was about to marry the man of my dreams and my parents were with me. Love just filled the room and I finally felt that my life was complete. Well, the only thing that was missing was Mrs. Carrie and Mr. Mack, but I knew they were in heaven smiling down on me.

Right then and there my father promised my mother to never let her out of his sight. He meant every word because he eventually closed his office in Sanford, Florida and opened a much larger office in Atlanta. He wanted his company to be a family affair, so I quit my job at AMX and started working for him. Now he was able to fly to Florida to see his mother who was still in a nursing home and also date Vivian. Finally, he asked her to marry him and she said yes. They had a small private ceremony on a beach in Jacksonville. It was a blessing from God that I was able to have my biological parents in my life.

I must have had a dreamy look on my face because right

then Lynda walked in the room and immediately said to me, "Penny for your thoughts."

"Good morning Lynda. I was sitting here thinking about old times. I'm so happy you came to see Brianna. The last time we were together it was three months ago at my baby shower."

"Girl, please don't talk about that. Remember that neighbor from Jacksonville? I think her name was Mrs. Williams. She was the belle of the party. She had all of us laughing so hard. Mom didn't like her because she kept the party alive. You know how Mom loves being the center of attention and she was left out completely."

"Yes, that was a great shower. Oh, speaking of Mrs. Williams, she passed away last month. The doctor wouldn't let me ride or fly there for her funeral, because of the stage of my pregnancy, but Mrs. Evyonne said it was a very nice and wasn't sad at all. She said all the neighbors had funny stories to tell about Mrs. Williams. We all know she would have wanted it that way- lively and not sad."

"Hey, have you heard from Christa and Monica?"

"They're both doing great. Christa took a principal's job in Orlando. Monica is still a happily married lady living in Jacksonville. We talk often and they promised to come up to see the baby before she starts walking."

We both laughed. "How did Christa end up in Orlando?"

"If you didn't notice at my baby shower Christa had put on the pounds and had been feeling a little unwanted. She started spending a lot of time on the internet in one of those chat rooms talking to a man name Bryan. She found herself talking to him daily. The next news I got was that he wanted to meet her in person. Christa thought that would be a good idea and so they did. Monica said he started visiting Christa almost every weekend. After several dates she decided to put in some job applications and was offered a principal's job at one of the public schools in Orlando. Monica spilled the beans about Christa and Bryan planning to get married this summer."

"I've always been skeptical about chatting on the internet, but that seems to be the going thing these days. You just don't know who you are talking to or what kind of baggage they are bringing with them."

"Lynda, I feel exactly the same way. At first, all Monica would say was how nice Bryan was, but then she started saying each time he and Christa were in their company, Christa paid for everything. That didn't sit right with me. Then Monica told me how he had changed jobs a lot."

"You know she ought to think about running a background check on Bryan before marrying him. She may find out that she really doesn't know him well at all. The internet has a wealth of information and my suggestion is that she look up your local felons in her state. It's better to be safe than sorry."

"I think I'm going to put in a call to Monica to see what she thinks about my telling Christa about your idea."

Lynda looked around. Then she leaned over and whispered, "If you can keep a secret, I did a background check on Carlos. Call me skeptical but, I knew that I had fallen in love with him and wanted to know as much about him as I could. I don't have any regrets at all about doing this."

"Lynda, you are too much."

"I needed to be sure. It was bad enough Mom didn't like

him because he chose to be a mail carrier. She always thought I would marry an attorney or doctor. I married where my heart was. It wasn't about money or status, it was about love and me not being lonely anymore."

"How are things with Mother Liz and Carlos since little Carlos is in the picture?"

"Mom seems to be a little better. She knows that her opinion doesn't matter one bit to me. She loves that little boy. Oh, speaking of Mom, they are planning to visit you and Brandon soon. Dad is playing golf with some friends in Miami and thought he would come for a short visit and leave mom here while he played golf with his friends."

"That sounds good—then they can see Brianna."

"I'd better go back and check on little Carlos. He and his father should be getting up soon."

Lord, forgive me for lying to Lynda. It would be very nice to see Brandon's father, but his mother could easily stay home and look at the pictures that Brandon downloaded for them.

I went back in the room to check on Brianna; she was still sleeping. As I was walking down the hall I heard, "Linda, I'm coming in."

"Hi Mom, I was just checking on Brianna. She's still sleeping. Let me help you with these packages. Together we can get breakfast ready in no time at all. Lynda was just in here with me. She went to check on Carlos and her son."

"You look a little tired this morning. I can stay later than usual. I could keep Brianna and entertain Lynda and Carlos, while you go back and get some much needed rest."

"Brianna is still waking every two hours for feeding, but

Brandon is off today. He had a late night at the hospital, so he's still sleeping. When he gets up he can entertain them and watch Brianna if you have something to do."

"Linda I don't have any plans for today. I'll be here to help you until you get back to normal. You're my primary concern and I really don't want you to over do it."

"Mom, thanks for caring, but I'm getting stronger every day. Now let's get this breakfast ready before they're up and hungry. Speaking of being up, how was dad when you left?"

"Tired. He came in late, ate and then rushed to his office to do more work. I tell you all he does is work. I would like to make plans for us to take a vacation. One where he shuts the cell phone off and leaves the computer home!"

"When tax season is over, why don't you do just that. After Lynda and Carlos leave, come over and we'll surf the internet and put together a nice trip for you."

"It is going to be hard getting your father to pick up and leave. That man eats and sleep work. One good thing, though he does take care of his body by exercising three days a week. He is really keeping himself in tip- top shape."

"Mom, you don't do bad yourself. Brianna has a good-looking grandmother."

Mom stood in the middle of the kitchen with big smile.

"You go on back in the room with Brianna. Put your feet up and relax. I'll have breakfast ready in no time at all. Plus, you'll just be in my way if you stay."

"You don't have to tell me twice."

While walking to the family room, I started thinking about the conversation Lynda and I had about doing a background check on Bryan. Should I call Monica to tell her about my suggestion to do a background check on Bryan? Then the thought came to—what if we find out he has a felony? Then what? Should we tell Christa or keep it to ourselves? What kind of friends would we be letting her continue in a relationship with a known criminal? He would never be able to keep a job to support her. Oh my goodness, I need to pray. Should I call Monica? Should we get involved or just leave it alone? Oh Lord, please tell me what to do!

Chapter Two

Carlos walked in the kitchen with a big smile on his face. He rubbed his hands together and said, "Something smells awfully good coming from the kitchen and I'm hungry and ready to eat."

Carlos came over and gave me a warm and friendly hug and planted a big kiss on Brianna's head as he took a seat in the plush chair next to mine. He started talking about how beautiful the house was and how he could get used to sleeping in our well- decorated guestroom. I thanked him for the compliment. I told him that as soon as Brandon smelled the bacon he would be heading this way.

Just then, Brandon entered the room, gave Carlos a big hug and said, "I heard you talking about me. Now, where is that little man of yours?"

"He's dressed and now your sister is putting his shoes on. You should see him- he looks like a mini- me."

Lynda walked in well dressed from head to toe. She was sporting a lime green short sleeved pantsuit with the same shade of flat shoes. Brandon turned to greet her. He said, "Hey, Sis you look good." He then reached out and gave her a big hug. Carlos Jr. was in her arms just looking at Brandon.

He reached for little Carlos, but little Carlos didn't want to leave his mother's arms. Brandon said "Come to your uncle and let me see you. Can he walk?"

"Brandon, you know he's only 10-months old. He walks around the furniture, but he hasn't let go. Where's the highchair mom brought for Brianna? May I use it so Carlos can sit and eat at the table with us?"

"Sure, you may use it. It will be quite a while before we'll need it, but we assembled it anyway. It's in the nursery in a corner with her other gifts that she can't use just now. You know if mom came and didn't see the highchair she bought, there would be lots of questions and mom would definitely feel unappreciated."

Lynda, said, "And you know we wouldn't want to upset the 'queen'."

Brandon didn't comment as he just left the room to get the highchair. Lynda leaned over and whispered, "Is Brandon okay? He looks a little tired and like he has lost a few pounds."

"I guess because I see him every day I hadn't noticed. Last night he had a long night at the hospital and that happens from time to time, but other than that he's doing great."

"By the way, I forgot to tell you I love your new home. You know the last time we were here you were still moving things in. You've really outdone yourself on decorating this beautiful home."

"Thanks. I can't take the credit for the decorating. I hired one of Atlanta's finest and she did an excellent job. I sure hope your mother is pleased when she comes to visit. I sent her some pictures, but now that it's completed, I hope she likes it."

"Look this is your place. Don't let her come here telling you how to decorate your home. She can either stay here with you and Brandon and be comfortable or take her judgmental attitude to the nearest hotel. I remember when she came to stay a week after little Carlos was born. She was more trouble than help. I wanted her to leave so badly. She and Carlos got along well."

Carlos said, "Yes and that's because I stocked the pantry and refrigerator with plenty of her favorite wine. She was drinking so much she forgot about not liking me."

"Carlos, you should be ashamed of yourself. You're talking about my mother as if I'm not even in the room."

"Baby, you know I am not lying about your mother, Mother Liz. And Linda, if you want her visit to be a good one I suggest you have Brandon stock your house with her favorite wine."

"But we don't drink."

"You want peace don't you? Then I suggest you buy plenty of wine."

Everyone started laughing at what Carlos said about Mother Liz. As I was about to comment on what he said, mom walked in and told us breakfast was being served in the formal dining room.

Brandon reached for the carrier to take Brianna in the dining room; when he lifted it, she started moving a little. The next thing we noticed her eyes were wide open. She looked around and let out a loud cry. I told Brandon to go on and eat and that I would be in later after taking care of her. He wanted to stay and help, but I insisted that he go in and entertain his sister and brother-in-law.

After Mom got everyone settled in the dining room, she came in the nursery to assist with Brianna. I told her we were fine. She wanted me to pump some milk for later, so she could feed her while I rested. I didn't want to hurt her feelings, so I told her after Brianna's feeding I would pump some milk and put it in the refrigerator. Mom stood there watching and smiling. Her gestures let me know that she was going to be a wonderful and loving grandmother.

After taking care of Brianna and pumping the milk, I was so hungry for a plate of food. I walked into the dining room to see that everyone was finished eating and all the food was removed from the table. They were laughing, talking and drinking coffee.

Brandon reached for Brianna so I could eat. I followed Mom into the kitchen to where the food was. I certainly didn't expect the spread that was on the counter top waiting for me! She had fried potatoes, scrambled eggs, pan sausage, bacon, biscuits and gravy, fresh fruit, and cinnamon rolls.

I turned around, gave her a big hug and a kiss on the cheek. "Mom you really did it up. Now, what are we having for dinner?"

"For dinner Linda, you and Brandon better think of something. While I was cooking I was thinking about taking your father to a movie and dinner so he could relax if he isn't too tired."

While I was fixing my plate I looked over and noticed mom was running water over the dirty dishes. "Mom, please don't worry about the dishes. Come on in the dinning room and visit with us."

"You go on in there; I'll load the dishwasher first. I'll be right in."

"Thanks again, Mom, for making breakfast."

"You don't have to keep thanking me. That's why I'm here—to help out."

No sooner had I walked in the dining room when I heard Carlos still talking about Mother Liz and her favorite wine.

I said, "Brandon, did you know your parents were coming for a visit either this coming weekend or the next?

"This is news to me. I just heard about the visit from Carlos. I was sitting here thinking about leaving mom with you while I played a little golf with dad in Miami with his friends."

"Brandon, please don't leave me here with your mother. I know we'll clash about how I'm taking care of our new baby. It's bad enough that I'll have to hear about how the house is decorated, when she arrives."

"You all stop being so hard on Mom. You make her out to be some kind of a monster."

Lynda and Carlos said it at once, "She is" and everyone but Brandon started laughing. Anyone could tell Brandon is such a mama's boy.

Mom came in wanting to know why we were laughing. Carlos started telling her about Mother Liz. How she was a lady who could easily make the society page of the daily newspaper. He went on and on about her being on a high horse and said that one of these days someone or something is going to knock her off her throne.

Mom said, "I know how you feel Carlos and it isn't good for someone to treat you like you are less than desirable. God made us all for a purpose. Not everyone can be a professional.

I feel like someone has to own the company and some have to do the laboring. This reminds me about what happened between Alphonso and I. We were teenagers and very much in love. His parents didn't want him to date or love anyone from the old neighborhood. His mother especially wanted him to keep his head in the books and go to college. She wanted him to meet some wealthy girl and live happily ever after. I know because while Alphonso and I were secretly dating, he would tell me how she felt about the girls in the neighborhood. When I got pregnant with Linda, my parents marched me to their house across the street. All hell broke loose. His parents wanted nothing to do with me and said their son was going to college. She had plenty of suggestions for me such as leave town, or place the baby for adoption. And her last statement was for me to never step foot on their property again."

Mom started coughing like she was getting all choked up with her feelings, but she didn't let that stop her. She reached for her water, took a sip, and continued.

"When my parents sent me to Jacksonville to live I felt like they kind of disowned me. It was sad at first, but God had a plan and I was able to take care of my children and make it. I said children because Linda had a sister but she died. She was hit by a car while playing in the street."

Carlos was all ears. He just had to interrupt mom's story. He said, "I'm sorry you have to bring up old memories about losing a child, but please tell me what happened when you came face- to- face with her at the wedding. Did she treat you nice?"

"Yes, we were nice to each other because it was Linda's

day. Shortly after that, Alphonso came to Jacksonville for a visit. He asked if I was willing to ride back to Sanford with him to meet with his mother. I was about to say no, when he said she asked him to bring me there to see her."

Mom was about to complete her story when little Carlos started crying. He was wet and wanted his diaper changed. Lynda asked mom to wait until she got back to continue her story.

Lynda returned in no time and asked mom to finish her story. Mom said, "I didn't want to visit her, but she asked so I went. When we arrived at the rehabilitation center, it was beautiful. Alphonso signed us in. While we waited in the lobby for her to be wheeled in, I looked out the window and couldn't help but notice the well- manicured landscape and beautiful outdoor furniture on the grounds. The place looked like a five star resort, not a rehabilitation center."

"I was nervous and scared at the same time. I prayed all the way down there and was still praying while I was standing in the lobby. Alphonso kept asking if I wanted to sit and the only excuse I could think of was no, I sat in the car all the way there. Actually, I was too scared to sit. I felt like standing was a good option for me. If she said anything I didn't like, all I had to do was run out the front door and wait for him at the car."

Everyone thought that was so funny. As I looked over, all eyes were on Mom. They were hanging on her every word. She was telling her story and putting her feelings into it.

"Finally, Mrs. Banks was escorted into the room. I stood there not knowing what to do. I didn't know if I should smile, frown, or just plain faint. By now I could actually feel my knees knocking. I took a deep breath and wondered if I should hug her or just knock her out of that wheelchair for keeping us apart most of our lives."

Mom took a breath and was about to finish her story when little Carlos wanted his dad to pick him up and then kept asking for a drink. Carlos was on the edge of his seat. He didn't want to leave the room. He didn't want to miss any of this story, he had to know what happened at that visit. He blurted out, "Lynda please go into the kitchen to get little Carlos bottle or sippy cup. I don't want to leave this room. I need to know what happened next.

When she looked at you, did she have a smile or a frown on her face? Please tell me who said the first word, was it you or Mrs. Banks? This is too good- I need to know what happened next."

Chapter Three

The telephone started ringing off the hook. Brandon answered and it was dad calling mom. Carlos was still sitting and waiting to know what happened next. Mom took the call and when she hung up, she said "Carlos, I know you want to know what happened, but that was Alphonso. He wants me to meet him at the rehabilitation center right away."

"Mom, did anything happen to grandmother?"

"Yes, it sounds as if she either fell out of bed or her wheelchair. I'll know more when I get there."

Brandon was so nice and concerned. He asked "Do you want me to drive you there?"

"No, I don't think it's that serious and I'm okay to drive, but thanks. Carlo, I don't mean to keep you hanging with the story, so here's the short version. She apologized, I accepted it and now we seem to get along very well. Linda, I'll let you know about your grandmother. Brandon, you and Carlos have a good day and I'll see you later."

Brandon leaned over and kissed me gently on the lips. He said since mom didn't need him to drive her to the rehab center, he and Carlos were on their way to play nine holes of golf.

Lynda left the room and returned with her purse and little Carlos' backpack. She looked at me and said, "Linda, you get some rest and Carlos make sure you play the full nine holes because we are going to have some fun today. I'll probably get a pedicure, that way I can hold little Carlos on my lap while my feet are being worked on. I know he won't sit still long enough for me to get a manicure. Anyway, I'll see you later."

"Not before giving me a kiss. Come here little Carlos and let daddy give you a big hug and a kiss too."

Brandon grabbed his golf clubs and headed toward the car. Brianna and I followed him out to the garage. We stood there looking and I waved bye bye. Lynda picked up little Carlos and rushed passed us, but not without saying how she wished I could be with them on this bright and shiny day.

I was glad to now have the house all by myself because I was really tired and sleepy. I looked at Brianna and said, "Little girl, it's our time to take a long nap and I mean more than one or two hours."

I woke up to the sound of Brianna crying from a distance. My first thought was that Brandon wanted me to rest so he took her to the nursery to change and feed her. I got out of bed, put my feet into my waiting soft slippers and headed to the nursery only to find it wasn't Brandon holding and feeding her. It was mother.

"Mom, what are you doing back here? How is grandmother?"

"She's okay, just being fussy and hateful as ever. When the nurse was trying to get her out of the bathtub, Grandma slipped back in. Thank God she didn't hit her head or anything."

"Did dad suggest they take her to the hospital to be checked out?"

"No, this kind of thing has happened before. I really think she wants us to take her out so she can move in with us, but I can't handle her by myself."

"How did you get in? What time is it?"

"Brandon gave me a key because I told him I wanted to come back to help out. I think it's around 5 o'clock."

"You mean Brandon and Carlos are still on the golf course?"

"Yes, and Lynda and little Carlos are still gone. It's just us here. Did you rest pretty well?"

"Yes, I did. I thank you so much for taking care of Brianna."

"You know, holding her and talking about Ann this morning brought up some old memories. Not a day goes by that I don't think about her. I also think about what a terrible mother I was to you when the accident happened."

"Mom, please don't bring that up. Not now. This is a new year and all of that is in the past and I forgive you. You weren't as strong in the Lord as you are now. Instead of holding onto God you held onto a bottle. I'm just thankful to God that the prayers of Mrs. Carrie, Mr. Mack and me helped you. I am happy about the relationship between us and that's all that matters now. Again, I forgive you completely so now is the time for you to forgive yourself."

"You're right. I need to let that chapter in my life be closed and learn from it. I am happy that your father and I are together. Some people don't get a second chance and God has given me second, third and fourth chances. Your father has accepted me unconditionally and that shows love. I do wish Mrs. Carrie was around to see this fine baby. She would be smiling and laughing all at the same time."

"You know she would be opening her Bible and reading Brianna scripture after scripture so that when Brianna got older she would know them by heart. Mrs. Carrie was good for everyone she came in contact with."

"You can say that again. Even though she had to take care of you, she never turned you against me. She always made it plain that I was your mother and she wanted us to be a family again."

"Yes she did."

This talk made me start to feel a little sad. I could actually feel tears welling up in my eyes. I don't know what my life would have been without Mrs. Carrie and Mr. Mack. God had a plan for me. I'll always be grateful to Him for having my life turned out the way it did. If not for Mrs. Carrie and Mr. Mack I probably would have been lost or put into foster homes. I wouldn't know the scriptures and the wisdom that I learned from them. I looked up and moved my lips so Mom couldn't see and said, "Lord, I thank you."

I could hear Brandon shouting down the hall. "Hey, Linda we're back from playing golf."

"Brandon, we're in the nursery with Brianna."

Brandon walked in, kissed me and gave me a big hug. He went over and kissed Brianna's head. He told mom that after he washed his hands he would be back to hold and spoil his little girl for a while.

Carlos came in looking for Lynda and little Carlos. I told him they weren't back yet. I also told him I was going to order some takeout for dinner.

The door bell rang, so I left Mom in the nursery to see if it was Lynda. I looked out- it was my dad. He was carrying a box and there was another box sitting on the porch.

"Hi, Dad, how are you?"

"Here take this box and I'll get the other one."

"What is all of this?"

"I know you have company and are in no shape to go out for dinner so I brought dinner for all of us. I called your mother and she told me what to bring."

Mom had given Brianna to Brandon and came into the kitchen. Dad took her in his arms and gave her a big kiss. It did my heart good to see the love between them.

"Linda, you set the table while I put the food in serving dishes."

"I can do that. Dad, thank you for doing this for us."

"Linda, you don't have to thank your old man. I wanted to do something for you while Lynda and Carlos were in town."

Just as I finished setting the table, Lynda and little Carlos came in. She said they went shopping and visited a friend, and while she was visiting, little Carlos took a nap. I told her "Dad brought dinner so get washed up and meet us in the dining room."

Dad went to one of my favorite restaurants and spared no expense. He brought ribs, steaks, potatoes, salads, rolls and desserts.

Carlos was the first one to the table. He was in rare form—laughing and bragging about how he beat the pants off Brandon in golf. Brandon walked in with Brianna in his arms not saying much, but the look on his face showed he was dead tired.

Brandon took a seat and then looked over at Carlos saying, "Man, I was just trying to show you a good time and not beat you this time, but when I come to Chicago I'll show you that I do have game."

Carlos laughed and so did Brandon.

Dad walked into the family room with a big smile on his face. He was looking at Brianna. He asked Brandon if he could hold her until mother called us to the table.

Brandon gave dad the little princess and said, "How's grandmother?"

Dad said, "She can be a handful sometimes. She can get hateful and start yelling at the staff. She acts up something terrible. I think she does this so that they would call me. When I go out there, she's a different person. She usually greets me with a warm and friendly smile. I think she wants me out there every day, but I have a business to run and I absolutely can't move her into our home because Vivian can't lift her. Anyway, to answer your question, she's okay."

"I heard you both talking about golf, Brandon, did you take Carlos to the Country Club?"

"Yes, and he loved it. When my parents come here in a week or two I'll probably make plans to take my father for a game or two. Do you think you would like to join us?"

"I would love too. Just call me the day before and I'll make arrangements to meet you here, so we can ride together. I'll even ask my friend Rod to come along. Rod and I play whenever we can get a few holes in. If I'm telling the story, then I am a better golfer. If Rod's telling the story, then he's the better golfer of the two of us. Anyway, I would love to invite him. That is, if it's okay with you?"

"Okay with me. Dad, I would love for Rod to golf with us. Then we all can see who plays the best."

Mom called us to the table to eat. We took our seats and dad asked us to join hands while he prayed over dinner. This setting did my heart good- having family members eating, talking and laughing together. My thoughts went back to Mr. Mack. He would always be the one to take us to the throne of grace. He was a thoughtful man. Mrs. Carrie loved to cook, but sometimes he would just tell us to get dressed, that he was taking his two best girls out to dinner. What was so special was that he would let me pick the restaurant most of the time. They were both good people and were really good about making me happy. Even though I am now blessed with my father, I can't help but think about how much of a father Mr. Mack was to me. This occasion makes me long so much for them.

Chapter Four

Three weeks had passed and things were back to normal. Brandon was back to work, but putting in long hours covering for two of his partners who were on mini vacations with their families. Mom was still coming over and helping for a few hours. Our maid, Essie, was cleaning two days a week. She changed the days to Tuesday and Friday. Brianna was 6- weeks old and seemed to be sleeping longer.

I looked out the window to see the sun shining bright. Brianna was asleep. This gave me a chance to do some computer work. Dad had given me the choice of either physically returning to work or working from my home until Brianna was about 6 months old. I opted to work at home.

I went into my home office to log on my computer. I was in the mood to finally get some work done. I had nice soft gospel music flowing throughout the house via the intercom. I was feeling good now. As I sat in my office chair to answer some emails, there was a message from the guard shack, "Mrs. Alexander, are you expecting company?"

I got up and pressed the intercom. "No."

"There is a couple here by the name of Dr. Winston and Elizabeth Alexander."

I threw both hands in the air. I couldn't believe what I had just heard. If I didn't answer, he won't let them in. I cleared my throat and said, "Please let them in. Thank you."

The Alexanders! Why in the world wouldn't they have called to let me know they were coming today? Essie doesn't come until tomorrow. Just as I was about to scream, the phone started to rang.

"Linda honey, Mom just called to let me know they are arriving here today. I'll be home a little late so you are kind of on your own."

"I know. I just got a call from the guard. They're here now. I'll have Mom come over and stay with the baby while I get some dinner. See you when you get home."

"Linda, I love you."

"Thanks."

Why in the world didn't they call this week to let me know they were on their way? I don't feel like entertaining Mother Liz. If I knew they were coming I would have been walking through the house anointing it with oil and praying in every room. I'm in no way ready for this. Oh God, give me strength to deal with this lady.

I'm not even dressed for company. I have on a pair of jeans and an old red and white blouse with tan bedroom slippers. My hair, oh my God, my hair is in a ponytail and it really needs to be washed. Darn! There's the door bell.

As soon as I opened the door, Mother Liz was standing there with her hands stretched straight out. I thought she was going to greet me with a hug. She looked right past me and said, "Oh Linda, where is my grandbaby? I just want to wash my hands, hold her and kiss those little rosy cheeks."

I moved to one side and pointed down the hall saying, "Come on in and I'll show you to your bedroom and then to the nursery." Daddy Alexander was nice as usual. He reached and hugged me and kissed me on the cheek. I don't know how he has stayed married to this inconsiderate lady for so many years.

Mother Liz rushed into the guest bathroom, then rushed into the nursery and picked up Brianna. She took a seat in my rocking chair and just drooled all over her granddaughter. She kept saying how beautiful Brianna was and how she looked just like her dad. I know that, but she does have the same shape face and forehead as mine.

I left them in the nursery and rushed to call Mom to ask if she wanted to come over while I went to pick up some dinner.

I called Mom. Her telephone rang three times and just as I was about to hang up, she answered. "Mom, Brandon's parents are here and I have no dinner prepared. Will you come over and sit with them while I call somewhere for dinner?"

"Why don't you just call it in and your father and I will pick it up. We would love to join you all for dinner."

"Great, I'll call it in and pay you when you get here. Mom, thanks so much."

"What are you going to do for breakfast? How long are they staying anyway?"

"I really don't know at this time. I'll ask so I can do some shopping."

"Okay, you call it in, we'll pick it up and be right over. See you soon."

"Thank you so much."

I went back into the nursery where Brandon's Mom and Dad were fussing over Brianna. She was all smiles with them. I told them we could go into the family room. I also told them that my parents would be joining us for dinner. No sooner had the words come out my mouth when Mother Liz asked Daddy Alexander if he had brought in her wine.

I wanted so much to say that we don't drink in this house, but didn't. Daddy Alexander went to the guestroom and came back with a large bag full of bottles. He asked if he could put them in the refrigerator so they would be nice and cold for dinner. I wanted him to be comfortable and told him the kitchen is still in the same place.

Mother Liz took Brianna in her arms and headed into the family room. She was looking at the pictures on the wall while she was walking. I was behind her, watching her head moving from side to side.

"Linda, you have done a lot with this house. It's simply beautiful. I sure hope my son isn't in too much debt trying to live out here in Alpharetta with the rich and famous."

I didn't know if I should have commented or not, so I didn't say a word. I wanted to say, "I work too and I make a 6- figure income just like Brandon." I also wanted to tell her that I sold my condo, which helped put a down payment on this house, but I didn't. I just walked on into the family room without answering her. If she makes that comment again, then I am not going to act like I didn't hear her, but I'm going to set her straight.

When we all gathered in the family room, I asked them how they liked their steaks cooked. Daddy Alexander said medium-well. Mother Liz said the same. She then got smart and asked if I would be putting them on the grill? I told her no, that I didn't know they were coming, so I was ordering from a restaurant and had asked my parents to pick it up.

Mother Liz is starting to get on my last nerve and she hasn't even been here an hour! She said, "What would you have done if we were not here? My son works hard and needs a well-balanced meal when he comes home from work."

Before I answered I said, "Lord please speak through me. I don't want to be disobedient to this petite lady with a big mouth, but I do need to let her know that I am not starving her son." I took a deep breath and said, "I would have warmed up the casserole in the refrigerator and made him a fresh tossed salad with a dinner roll."

"Well, do you have enough for the four of us? I hate that you're putting your parents to all this trouble just for us."

"No Mother Liz, there isn't any trouble at all. Mom and Dad would love to sit and chat with you and Daddy Alexander."

I went into the kitchen to order the food. Daddy Alexander was in there trying to find a glass so he could pour Mother Liz a tall glass of wine. I helped him to find one of our fancy glasses. I told him it wasn't a wine goblet, but it was all we had. He said that either she could drink out of the glasses we had or the bottle. We both laughed, but not too loud.

Brianna finally went to sleep in Daddy Alexander's arm. I thought I would give his arm a rest, so I took her to her in her crib. While walking back to the family room I overheard Mother Liz asking Daddy Alexander if he had seen the backyard. She didn't hear me coming down the hall because I heard her say, "They've even got a small pond and I bet there are all kinds of tropical fish in there. I think Brandon is trying to keep up with those other doctors or else Linda is trying to make him think she is used to expensive things. You know this house cost a fortune."

She looked up and saw me and all she could do was put the glass of wine to her lips. I wanted to tell her that I had heard the entire conversation. Lord, I don't know what I'm going to do when Daddy Alexander leaves for his golf trip in Miami. When he returns, I'll be the one with a wine glass walking from room to room.

I went to turn on the TV, but Mother Liz stopped me. "Linda come, sit down and let's talk. Please tell me how things are with you and my only son."

"Brandon is working as usual. His practice is growing and they are thinking about interviewing for another partner. I am so very proud of him. He's a great father to Brianna and a loving husband to me. I can't ask for anything else. My life is happy."

"Linda, while I was in the kitchen I saw a schedule on the refrigerator. Who is Essie?"

"Essie is our maid. She will be here tomorrow. You will get to meet her."

"No I won't. We're going downtown and to visit a friend of mine who just moved here a month ago."

"Then I think Brianna and I will visit my grandmother. That way I won't be in Essie's way while she cleaning."

"In her way? This house is so big you can be sitting in the front while she cleans the back."

"You're right. I was just making an excuse to get out for a while. My grandmother hasn't seen the baby yet. It's better for me to take her there, than for my grandmother to come here."

Just as I was about to make some more small talk, I heard the side door opening. I excused myself and rushed to help my parents, but it wasn't them. It was Brandon.

"Brandon, you're home early?"

He kissed me and said, "From the expression on your face, not early enough. Where are my lovely parents?"

"They're in the family room."

Brandon walked in and rushed to his mother first. She got up and gave him a big hug. She said, "There goes my baby. How are you doing? Look at you! You work so hard you don't get to eat. Brandon you're so skinny. Honey, doesn't Linda feed you?"

"Mom, stop it! I don't work any harder than Linda. I know I have lost a few pounds and I plan to take a physical real soon. You know doctors make the worst patients. Dad, come here and give me one of those bear hugs I'm used to getting from you. Dad, you really look well. I wish I could fly to Miami and play a little golf with you, but this isn't a good time. I'll catch you when I come home for a visit."

"Brandon, Brianna is so cute. She looks just like you did when you were a baby. I used to take you out and with all that hair you had on that tiny head, people thought you were a pretty little girl. They didn't notice all the blue I had you dressed in."

"Son, your mother is right. Brianna is such a beautiful angel given to us by God. Are you and Linda going to have anymore children?"

"Wait Dad, wait until we get this one walking and potty trained."

We were all laughing at that. I told them I was going to the kitchen. This can give Brandon some quality time with his parents. I'm going to set the table and get the serving dishes ready for the food when Mom and Dad arrive with it.

I was putting the glasses on the table when I heard a car. It was Mom and Dad. As I ran to the door to let them in, I said to myself, "Boy am I glad to see you." Dad had a large box and Mom had two small boxes in her hands. "Hey guys, I'm sure glad to see you. Did you get a steak for Brandon? He came home early and you know he likes his steak cooked like mine—"Well Done."

Mom said, "We knew he had to come home some time, so yes, we included him. Oh, guess what? Your dad and I had a conversation while riding over and came up with a great idea to take the Alexanders to breakfast in the morning. Then you and Brianna can sleep in and relax."

"Thanks Mom, but they've made plans to go downtown and to visit some friends. I even made plans to take Brianna to visit grandmother tomorrow. Mom, will you go with us?"

"Yes, do you want me to come here or will you pick me up?"

"I don't feel like changing the base of the car seat, so we'll pick you up."

Mom and Dad followed me into the family room where everyone was sitting. I asked where Brandon was and was told he went into the nursery to get Brianna. He heard her crying.

Mom and Dad greeted the Alexanders with hug and kisses. Brandon returned with Brianna and Dad automatically reached for her. He said, "Come to Papa, my little angel, you have grown since last week."

By this time Mother Liz had several glasses of wine. She shouted almost at the top of her lungs at my Dad, "Aren't you going to wash your hands before you pick her up? You just came in from outside with all those germs."

The tone she used was quite rude! Everyone looked at her. We couldn't believe what she had said. I got a little nervous because my mom is usually nice, but if provoked, she can be a force to be reckoned with. I was thinking, "These are the people who went out of their way to bring us a nice dinner and now you're being rude to them." Mother Liz didn't know if my father had washed his hands or not. The atmosphere in the room went from friendly to tense in less than a second.

Chapter Five

Brandon's father flashed a look at Mother Liz that made me sit up and notice that he was sick and tired of her smart mouth too. Mother Liz must have seen that look because instead of putting her glass on the crystal coaster, she put it down on the glass table and with a smirk look on her face she said, "Alphonso, I owe you an apology, please forgive me. I know you wouldn't do anything to hurt our grandbaby. You did hear me say <u>our</u>."

Dad smiled back and said she was right- he should either wash his hands or use hand sanitizer before handling Brianna. Brandon picked up the hand sanitizer that's kept in the family room and handed it to dad. I was speechless, so Mom said, "Please excuse us, Linda and I will unpack the food and get it ready."

I couldn't get into the kitchen fast enough. I was steaming and furious. Mom looked at the expression on my face and before I could say a word, she said, "Honey you know how she is, so please don't let her get under your skin. Remember you only have to deal with her for a few days. Thank God she doesn't live with you."

"Mom, you're right. I can take it for the next few days. I'll just keep praying God will give me strength for this journey."

"That's my girl. Now let's get this food on the table."

We heated everything and put it in dishes and then called everyone to the dining room for a tasty meal. I could tell they were hungry because we didn't have to call them twice. Brandon was the first one in the room and everyone followed right behind him. He stood at the head of the table, and offered my dad a seat. Then he walked to the other side to sit next to me. I don't know if he felt bad about his mother's comment, but it made me feel good to have my father and Brandon's father sitting at our end of the table.

Brandon asked his father to say grace. Daddy Alexander asked us to hold hands while he prayed over the food. In his prayer he thanked God for the food, and prayed for our safety and health. He ended his prayer by thanking God for blessing us with a precious little girl. We all said, "Amen!"

Dinner was good and the conversation went well. Dad talked about his business and Brandon's father talked about retirement and about one of his favorite subjects and that was golf. My Mom didn't say much; she just enjoyed her steak. Mother Liz did little talking, all while enjoying her second or third glass of wine.

After the dinner everyone headed for the family room. Dad looked at his watch and said, "Vivian and I are going to call it a night. Linda said you two will have a long day tomorrow. We will probably see you again before you leave."

Mother Liz said her goodnights and went down the hall toward the guest room. Daddy Alexander shook Dad's hand and thanked him again for such a delicious dinner. He also apologized about Liz's rude comment about him picking up the baby without washing his hands. My dad accepted his apology and told me that he would talk to me tomorrow.

I left Brianna with Brandon and Daddy Alexander as I walked my parents to the car. I thanked them again for dinner. I reminded mom of the visit tomorrow with grandmother. She said she would be ready and that I should call her just before leaving the house.

I went back inside to clean the kitchen, but not before going into the family room to see if Brandon needed anything. When I walked in, the family room was empty. I went to the nursery and found Brandon changing Brianna's diaper. I just stood in the doorway and smiled. I walked back to the kitchen to fill the dishwasher and tidy up just a little. I was glad Essie would be here in the morning to clean the house.

After a restless night, I was just about to fall into a deep sleep when Brandon said,

"Good morning, Linda, I'm going to put Brianna in bed with you while I take my shower. You don't have to worry about getting up to fix breakfast. I plan to go in a little early today. I'll call you this afternoon."

"Okay, see you, Baby. Have a good day."

I was in a deep sleep when Brianna made a little noise. I woke up and looked at her, but she was still asleep. She must have been dreaming. Then I started looking around. I took in a few deep breaths and said to myself, "No. I smell food?" I propped several pillows around Brianna and went down the hall to see what Brandon was doing in the kitchen when he was supposed to be at work.

"Good morning Linda, you didn't know I knew my way around a kitchen, did you?"

I rubbed my eyes to make sure it was Mother Liz standing in what took like a pair of two inch wedged satin heels with gold flowers on the top. She even had the nerve to be wearing my favorite apron with the smiling face.

I said, "Good morning Mother Liz, you have it smelling really good in here. After I wash my face and freshen up, may I help you while Brianna is still sleeping?"

"Yes, you can set the table. There will be five of us."

"Five?"

"Yes, I called your parents and asked them to please join us for breakfast."

"I take it by your saying five, they accepted the invitation."

She had the nerve to spin around and say, "Why yes, why wouldn't they?"

Either she had too much wine or she is plain crazy. She knew she upset my father last night. Maybe this was her way of making it up to him.

I smiled and said, "Mother Liz, you asked why wouldn't they? I guess because Dad and Mom wanted to take you both to breakfast, but I told them you had plans for today."

"Why my dear Linda, we do have a full day, but not this morning. Our plans are to get together with friends after breakfast."

"Sorry I misunderstood. I'll be right back to help you with breakfast."

I couldn't get out of there fast enough. I had to freshen up and have a little talk with Jesus. This lets me know that she does have a conscience. Either that or Daddy Alexander chewed her out when he reached the bedroom.

After dressing Brianna and myself, I was on my way

to the kitchen when the door bell rang. Daddy Alexander called that he would get it. I went back into the nursery to get Brianna who was sitting so nice and quiet in her carrier. She was dressed in her pink and white dress with matching pink sandals and didn't even make a fuss when I brushed her hair down flat and put a pink band around it.

By the time I brought her to the family room, both men were sitting and drinking cups of flavored coffee. Dad reached for the hand sanitizer, then reached for Brianna who was smiling like she really knew who he was. Just as I was about to head to the kitchen to be with the ladies, Essie was making her way in the back door.

"Good morning Essie, I would like to introduce you to my in-laws."

"Mother Liz, this is Essie."

Mother Liz shook her hand and gave her a welcoming smile. Essie knew Mom so she went to where my mother was standing and gave her a big hug.

"Essie, please follow me into the family room where Dad is and you can meet my father-in-law, Dr. Alexander."

Essie walked in and flashed a big smile at Daddy Alexander. She seemed to be friendly and nervous at the same time. I noticed that she rubbed her hands down her pants legs before extending her hand to shake his.

Essie looked at Daddy Alexander and said, "It's was very nice to meet you. Good to see you again, Mr. Banks."

She rushed off quickly. I followed her to the nursery and asked if there was something wrong. I noticed her hands were shaking.

Essie said, "Linda, I don't want you to think I'm fresh or

anything but Mr. Alexander looks just like my dead husband. My husband was tall, dark, and handsome just like him. I started to sweat just before I shook his hand."

"Essie I knew your husband was dead, but you never talked about how he looked."

"No, there was no reason to talk about how he looked until now. All I can say is he was handsome like Mr. Alexander!"

We both laughed. "Essie, where are my manners? Would you like to join us for breakfast?"

"Linda, I've eaten already and even if I hadn't, it would be too hard to me to eat and keep my eyes off that man. Thanks anyway. Boy, this man has really stirred up some fond memories. I'd better start cleaning. I'll start in the back and work my way to the front. No, I just got another thought, why don't I start in the family room?"

"Essie, you are too much. Thanks for making me laugh. We'll be out of your way in a little bit. After breakfast I'm taking Brianna to visit my grandmother and the Alexanders will be out all day visiting friends."

"Okay, I'll either see you later today or next week."

I went back to an empty family room. I heard the laughter coming from the dining room and walked in to find Dad holding and feeding Brianna.

Mom looked up and said, "I called you twice, but you never answered. Then I thought maybe you were going over some details with Essie."

"Yes, but now I am going to dive into this wonderful-looking breakfast."

Mom said, "You should try the omelets. They are light and fluffy, stuffed with ham, cheese, green peppers and onions."

I filled my plate with an omelet, hash brown potatoes, two sliced tomatoes and a bagel with plenty of cream cheese. I looked up and saw all eyes were on me.

I said, "It's okay, I'm breast feeding. Therefore, I should eat a little more than usual."

Mother Liz said "Eating like that, you'll never get that baby fat off."

By this time I wanted to come back with a smart remark, so I just put my head down and said grace over my meal.

Mom understood how I felt because she got up from the table and took Brianna from Dad with the excuse that she was going to see if Brianna needed her diaper changed.

Mother Liz excused herself, by saying she was going to freshen up her make up and change her clothes. Daddy Alexander got up and told my dad how good it was to see him again and told him that he was going to get himself together so they could go visit their friends.

Dad reached over and poured himself another cup of coffee, while I tried to eat. He started making idle conversation about the job. He even spoke of the new clients that came aboard within the last two weeks. I wanted so badly to correct him. He must have forgotten that he emailed all their credentials to me to enter into the system.

I looked at him and tried to smile but my thoughts were not on his conversation. My thoughts were on that awful remark Mother Liz had said about my weight. I've never had a weight problem. Had she forgotten that I just gave birth to her grandchild? The only thing big on me is my stomach. I refuse to let that materialistic lady make me feel as if I look like the Goodyear blimp. Lord, when she comes back into this room, please help me to hold my tongue and not tell her off like I wanted to a long time ago!

Chapter Six

Mother Liz came into the kitchen stylishly dressed from head to toe. I don't know where these friends are taking her, but she'll be ready. She looked so nice in her designer black and white pantsuit. She even had on a pair of Versace slingback sandals with the matching purse. Daddy Alexander was sporting a linen black short sleeved shirt with a pair of linen black pants. Just as I was about to comment on how well they looked, Mother Liz opened her mouth.

"Linda, did your parents leave?"

"Yes, and they wanted to thank you again for the breakfast."

"It wasn't hard to prepare. I'm just happy we could all be together again. Oh, we've decided to spend the night with our friends. I tried to get out of it, but they just wouldn't take no for an answer. I'll be back around five tomorrow evening because Winston has to fly out at 8:00. Looks like it will be just you and me for the next two days."

She came over and gave me a big hug and said she would see me later. Daddy Alexander kissed me on the cheek and followed her to the car. That phrase kept ringing in my ear "you and me." I sure don't know what I'm going to do for the next two days.

I gathered up Brianna's things and walked over to the intercom to call Essie to let her know that I was leaving for most of the day.

"Essie, I'm leaving to visit with my grandmother. I'll see you later."

Later Essie's voice came through the intercom loud and clear "Okay, enjoy your visit."

Brianna and I went through the garage to the car. Setting her baby bag on the floor, I buckled her in the car seat. I put in my favorite gospel tape, took a deep breath and said to Brianna, "We are on our way to pick up your grandmother."

When we arrived, Mom was putting on the finishing touches of her makeup. I wanted to say that she was only going to visit Grandmother, but didn't say a word. I just sat there and waited for her to finish.

Mom got in the car wearing a nice red and white sun dress. I felt kind of under dressed wearing my Calvin Klein jeans. The ride to the rehabilitation center was quiet until I told Mom about Mother Liz staying with Brandon and I for the next two days.

Mom was looking straight out the window when she looked over at me and said, "Honey, remember she is visiting your house. You don't have to allow her to run over you. All you have to do is fall down on your knees and pray. You know that God talked in John 14:27 about peace. He said, 'Peace I leave with you, my peace I give unto you: not as the world giveth, give I unto you. Let not your heart be troubled, neither let it be afraid.'

"Mom, I'm not afraid of her. I just don't want Brandon and me to have a falling out because of her. She has a tendency to want things her way. I've also noticed that Brandon seems to be a mama's boy."

"Linda, mama's boy or not. He's your husband and I think he'll come to your aid and not allow her to start problems in your home. Just stay prayerful and watch God take care of it all."

"Mom, you just said a mouthful and the key word is 'prayer.' God hasn't brought me this far to leave me now. I also know that no matter what storm comes my way, God is still in control and He will carry me through."

"Amen!"

Mom and I just sat back and listened to the music while Brianna slept peacefully. All of a sudden my cell phone started to ring. I reached over and gave it to Mom to answer.

"Hello, Oh hi, Brandon. Linda is driving. We are on our way to visit mother. Do you want me to tell Linda anything?"

"Mom, please push the speaker button so we can hear each other."

"Linda, I'm calling to see what you want me to bring home for dinner?"

"Your parents will be spending the night with their friends, so it will be just you and me. We can order pizza when you come home."

"Okay, I'll see you around 6:00. Kiss Brianna for me. Mom, you take care and enjoy your visit."

"Thanks, Brandon."

"Mom, if you just fold the phone, it will hang up. Thank you for answering."

"Honey, Brandon is so considerate. He realizes you have your hands full with Brianna and still trying to do a little work from home. I am so happy you met and married this wonderful young man."

We pulled into the rehab center and I looked in the mirror to find Brianna still asleep. After parking I got her carrier unloosened from the base. The shaking and noise must have wakened her, because her eyes flew open real wide.

"Mom, why don't you go to the reception desk and let them know that we're here to visit with Grandmother. I'll take Brianna to the restroom to change her diaper."

"Okay, I'll meet you in the visiting room next to the lobby."

When I came out the restroom, Grandmother and mother were sitting in the visiting room chatting away. Grandmother had the biggest smile on her face. I rushed over and gave her a hug and kiss. She wanted to see Brianna so I took Brianna out of the carrier and placed her in Grandmother's arms.

"Oh Linda, I'm so happy God let me live to see another generation. This baby is just beautiful and precious."

"Thank you Grandmother. We are blessed to have her."

Grandmother's eyes started to fill with tears. Before long the tears were running down her cheeks. Mom reached for the baby while Grandmother wiped her eyes. I think we were all thinking the same thing. If my mother had aborted me like she really wanted, then there would not have been this precious gift from God.

The visit went well and we noticed Grandmother was getting tired. All of a sudden I thought Brianna had messed her diaper. I said, "Excuse me, but I think Brianna has messed on herself."

Grandmother was so embarrassed as she said, "Honey, I don't think it's Brianna. I have had this happen to me suddenly for the last couple of days. Please call my nurse to come and clean me up. I am so ashamed of myself. Please excuse me for the smell."

Mom was so sweet and said, "Mother, you don't have to worry the nurse. I'm willing to take you back to your room and clean you up. Linda doesn't mind waiting. We really have nothing to do but spend the afternoon visiting with you."

"No, Vivian, you don't have to do this. Please call my nurse and she'll be right up and take me back to be cleaned up. Thank you so much for wanting to help."

Mom went to the nurse station to put in a call for Grandmother's nurse. No sooner had mother returned, than a petite nurse with a warm and friendly smile came rushing to Grandmother's aid. She asked if we wanted to have something cold to drink while we waited. I said, "No, we'll be leaving."

"Grandmother, I promise to bring Brianna back for another visit."

"I sure hate that this happened. I enjoyed seeing her and both of you. Please don't tell my son about my little bowel problem. I think he worries about me too much."

"Grandmother, we won't. Your secret is safe with us."

Mom and I gave her a hug and left so the nurse could clean her up. When we got back into the car and before I drove off, I just had to say something to mom.

"Mom, you are really a Christian woman. Even though Grandmother was one of the people who kept you and Dad away from each other, you were willing to clean her up. I am so proud of you. Not many people would have done that."

"Linda, my thoughts were not on what she had done

to me in the past. My thoughts were like those little bands people used to wear 'What Would Jesus Do'. I am living for God, not man. When I die I want God to welcome me into the Kingdom of Heaven."

I drove on and before we knew it, we were pulling in the front of her house. I was looking for Dad's car, but it wasn't in the driveway. Mom looked at me and said, "Why don't you leave Brianna with me and treat yourself."

"Treat myself to what?"

"Treat yourself to a manicure and pedicure. You'll have enough time to get your hair washed and styled, too."

"Do I look that bad?"

"No, but this will give me a little time to spoil my grandbaby. You go on. We'll be okay. I'm going to call your dad and let him know Brianna is over here visiting. I bet he will rush home then. Like I said, you go on."

"If you insist, I'll do just that. I'll call Marilyn to see if she has an opening. If she does then I'll get my hair done. If not, then I'll just have that manicure and pedicure. Either way I know I'll probably feel better being pampered for a few hours. If you need me, just call my cell phone."

Chapter Seven

When I arrived at the shop Marilyn was waiting with a peculiar look on her face. I walked in and there were other ladies just sitting around talking, laughing, and drinking cold sodas.

"Hey Ladies, how's everyone today?"

Everyone spoke and Marilyn said, "Sit here so I can do something to this head of yours. Girl, you need a new hairdo. Why don't you look into these hair style books and find something new."

"Marilyn, why are you looking so mean today?"

One lady who was sitting under the last dryer yelled out and said "You mean you don't know?"

I looked at Marilyn and asked what was going on?"

Marilyn took a deep breath and said, "Linda, you know a beauty shop is where all the gossip is, so let me be the first to tell you. Philip and I are getting a divorce."

"A divorce! Marilyn, you have only been married to him four or five years. Please tell me what happened."

"I got fat and he lost interest, simple as that!"

"Do you think you could go to counseling to try and save your marriage?"

"I could, but his new girlfriend wouldn't like that."

"Oh Marilyn, I'm so sorry to hear this."

"Hey, don't worry. I'm getting stronger by the day. Now look in these two books and try to find something. You don't want Brandon to loose interest."

I didn't want to keep talking about the end of her marriage, so when she put the two books in my lap, I just turned the pages. The first book had nothing in it that I liked so I put it in the chair next to me and started looking through the second book.

Finally, I came across a hair style I liked. I called out to Marilyn. She came over and looked as if she had been crying a little. I acted as if I didn't notice her red eyes. I told her I thought I found what I wanted. I felt comfortable with her cutting my hair because she was a good stylist, and she could really cut hair.

"Now Linda, I know you don't want me to cut all your hair off. This style is short and you will have to wrap it nightly with a silk scarf."

"With me having Brianna now, I want something that won't take a long time to manage. I could wrap it nightly. The next morning unwrap it, run my hands through it and I'll be ready for the day."

"What will Brandon say about getting all your hair cut off? We're not talking about an inch or two. We're talking about cutting five or six inches of hair."

"I know, I think he'll like it. Let's do it."

"Speaking of Brianna, your mother showed us some pictures. Linda, she is a beautiful little girl with plenty of hair. Is she a good baby?"

"Yes, she doesn't cry a lot and that makes things smoother around the house. I've started working a little in my home office and it's like she isn't even there."

"Okay. Since you want the new short haircut, why not let Brenda do your makeup before you leave. That way you'll go home looking like a new lady."

"Okay, if Brenda doesn't mind. I have a pizza date with Brandon tonight. When he walks in, he'll be looking at a new foxy lady."

The room went quiet. Everyone was looking around at each other. I started to think just maybe I shouldn't have said that. Maybe Marilyn's husband left her for a young foxy lady.

One of the ladies, Cheryl, who was sitting in the corner getting a pedicure thought she would bring some life back into the place yelling, "That's what I'm talking about. You go on Church girl. I don't see anything wrong with your wanting to feel sexy for your husband."

This sparked a new conversation in the shop. The ladies started talking about how people used to wear their very best to church and now they walked in looking like after service they would be going to an all-night night club.

I didn't have a comment on the subject so I just sat there and waited for my turn to be pampered.

It seemed like I had been in there for four hours when it had only been two. I took out my cell phone and called Mom to check on Brianna. Mom said they were doing well together. She said Dad was there holding and spoiling her. I explained that I had my manicure and pedicure and how good my hands and feet looked and felt. I didn't have the heart to tell her that I just came from under the hair dryer.

She would wonder why it took such a short time to dry my hair. Little did she know that my hair was short now and cut so I could wear if off my face or style it forward.

Marilyn was ready to style my hair. I told mom I had to go and would see her in about an hour.

Marilyn styled my hair and Brenda applied the makeup. I looked like a new woman. I thanked everyone, took one more look in the mirror and asked Marilyn to please come outside for a minute.

When we got outside, I said, "Marilyn, you've always been a cheerful person, one who made people laugh and feel comfortable in your presence. Today, you were not that person. Don't let anyone take your joy. God speaks about crying in Psalm 30:5. 'Weeping may endure for a night, but joy cometh in the morning.' It's okay to cry, but do it only for a night. Look toward heaven and ask God to bring joy back into your life."

Marilyn laid her head on my shoulder and burst into tears. All I could do was to hold her all while saying, "God knows you are hurting, but He is the only one who can dry those tears. Please turn this situation over to Him."

Marilyn, dried her eyes and said, "You're right. I'm just not my old self and if I keep letting this make me bitter, then he wins. I'm just going to have to thank God that we didn't have any children, hold my head up and go on with my life."

"Now you're talking. You'd better go on back in the shop before that lady with the rollers in her hair decides to leave without paying you. She would have an advantage because she'll still have her money and free rollers."

Marilyn started laughing and thanked me for the

business and the chat.

I looked at my watch it was 5:00. I called Brandon to let him know that I was on my way to get Brianna and would be right home. The call went right into his voice mail. "Brandon, I'm on my way to pick up Brianna. If you get home before we do just order the usual, but this time add two small garden salads."

By now I was so hungry for some pizza, breadsticks, and salad. I hadn't eaten since breakfast except for a bag of chips and a coke.

When I arrived at Mom's house, Dad was getting out of the car. He looked up, waved at me and went on into the house with a grocery bag.

I walked in looking for mom. They were in the family room. Mom was feeding her. "Mom, did I stay away too long?"

"No, you just didn't leave enough milk. I remembered the name of that powered milk you had in your cabinet and sent your father to the store to get a small can. We were on the last bottle and I didn't want her to start crying. Hey, look at you! Where is my daughter?"

"Mom, do you like it?"

"Like it? I love your hair and your makeup is flawless."

"Mom you were right about pampering myself. I feel like a new woman."

Dad walked in to say hello. He looked at me and said, "Linda, you look so pretty. I thought your hair was in a ponytail. Now why did you cut your hair off?"

Mom came to my rescue, saying "Alphonso, it will grow back. I don't blame her for wanting to do something different with her hair. I like it and so will Brandon."

"You mean your husband hasn't seen you yet?"

"No Dad. I left the salon and came right over to get Brianna."

"Well, if he's anything like me, he is going to have a fit! I don't mind women cutting their split ends, but you cut it all off."

Mom said, "Well it was a good thing when you first saw me at Linda's wedding that I had a short hair cut. I feel I'm too old to have hair falling on my shoulders. I think I look younger with short hair."

We both looked at Dad to see what he had to say about that. "Vivian you are right. You look good, Baby, with short hair. Well, I have some work to do. Let me get a kiss from Brianna before you two leave. Linda, any time you want to rest or go out some where, please bring her over. We would love to keep her, she's such a good baby."

"Okay, Dad. Thanks for the offer."

Dad left the room in a hurry. Mom and I looked at each other and started laughing. We knew he wasn't going to say a word about Mom's hair. He was so happy to have her in his life that if she came home sporting a shaved head he would just smile all while asking her where the polish and a soft rag was so he could shine it for her.

Chapter Eight

Brianna and I got home and Brandon's car wasn't in the drive or garage. We went through the kitchen and there was a long dish covered in foil and a note sitting next to it on the counter. Essie had prepared her famous lasagna. Her note said the garlic bread was in the freezer and salad in the refrigerator. My mouth started to water just thinking about how she made it with lots of mozzarella, ricotta, and parmesan cheeses. Essie could make boiling water taste good! She was one of the best cooks in town. She even ended the note by saying how she hoped we all enjoyed it because she made plenty for everyone.

I didn't want to start eating before Brandon got home, so I had an apple instead. Afterwards I took Brianna to the nursery for a warm sponge bath. I planned to feed her and rock her to sleep just before Brandon came home.

My plans worked because just as I was placing her in the crib, I thought I heard the door. I turned around to find Brandon standing in the doorway flashing a big smile. I placed my finger to my lips, so he wouldn't say a word. He walked closer and put his arms around my shoulders. Now we were both looking down at our little precious gift from

God sleeping so peacefully.

We walked out and made it as far as the kitchen before Brandon turned and looked me straight in my eyes and said. "Why Mrs. Alexander, what have you done with yourself?"

"Brandon, from the gleam in your eyes, I think you like the new me."

"You'd better believe it. I love your hair cut and your makeup. Did you do all this just for me?"

"Yes, I figured you might have gotten tired of the "old me" walking around with my hair in a ponytail and looking like a plain Jane."

"I just figured since Brianna consumed all your time that you just hadn't had time or felt like doing much with yourself."

"After our visit with grandmother, I planned on coming home. Mom thought I should take this time and pamper myself. I left you a message on your voice mail."

"I got it and that's the reason I'm so late. I didn't need to rush home since you weren't here yet. What's that on the stove? I haven't called in the pizza yet."

"I'm glad you didn't. Essie made her favorite lasagna. She made enough for all of us. Since your mother and father won't be here tonight, why don't you go and wash up and I'll bring the food into the dining room."

"I'll be right back."

I put some garlic bread in the oven and put our salads on the table and placed two nice large slices of lasagna in the microwave to be heated. When everything was ready I went in the family room to get Brandon. He was sitting in his favorite chair with his feet up—sleeping.

"Brandon, dinner's ready. Come in the dining room."

"Oh Honey, I must have fallen asleep. I had the sports on and guess I just drifted off to sleep."

He followed me into the dining room where the food was on the table and the lights dimmed so we could eat by candle light.

Just as I was about to sit down, Brandon walked over and gave me a big kiss. He said, "Honey, did I tell you how good you look tonight?"

Through my blushing I said, "Yes, but it won't hurt for you to tell me again and again."

After dinner we went into the family room to watch TV. Well, I did the watching because I looked over and Brandon was fast asleep.

I woke Brandon and told him it was okay for him to go to bed. I wanted to watch the ending of a movie that was on Lifetime. I didn't have to tell him twice. Brandon left the room in a hurry.

After the movie ended I heard Brianna crying. I went into the nursery, fed and changed her. She wasn't ready to go back to sleep so I carried her to the family room to watch more TV until she fell back a sleep.

The next morning, I woke to find Brandon was gone and had left me a note on the dresser. It said, 'I'm going in early so I can get home a little early. You and Brianna were sleeping, so peacefully, I didn't have the heart to disturb you. See you later, Love Brandon'. I looked out and the sun was shinning bright. It was going to be a good day.

I turned on the intercom to listen to some of my favorite gospel songs. The music was piped through the house and put me in the mood for working. I picked up Brianna and went down the hall to my home office. Before long, Brianna was asleep and I was clicking away on my keyboard. I found myself singing along with the songs and working away. Just as I was finishing up my last spreadsheet, the telephone rang.

"Hello?"

"Linda, this is Monica how are you?"

"Monica, we're all are doing great. How are you and your family?"

"We're okay. How is Brianna?"

"Girl, you should see her. She's looking like a little round pound. The weight is settling in her cheeks. We are blessed that she isn't a cry- baby. Mom and I took her to see my grandmother and she acted like a perfect little angel."

"How are your parents?"

"They're doing great! Brandon's parents are here visiting."

"Oh my goodness, you mean that mother-in-law of yours is in town?"

"Yes, and guess what? She made breakfast for us."

"You mean she can cook? Are we talking about the same lady? You know the one who walks around looking down her nose at people."

"Yes, she can make a mean omelet. Okay here's the story: My parents were kind enough to bring dinner for everyone. Dad reached for Brianna and Mother Liz acted like he was contagious or something. She told him he needed to wash his hands before picking her up."

"How did your mother react? You know your father is so nice and sweet, but Vivian can get ugly if she's provoked."

"I know, and by the grace of God it didn't get out of hand."

"Tell me, have you heard from Christa?"

"Yes, there was a large library conference here in Jacksonville and Christa came with two of the librarians from her school. We went out to dinner a couple of times. All she talked about was Bryan. I asked her what she really knew about this guy and she got a little upset. She had the nerve to tell me she knew all she needed to know about him."

"It's funny you said that to her. I was thinking the same thing. Seeing how much weight she has put on, I think she's lonely and really relishes the attention he gives her. Has she tried to lose any weight?"

"Linda, I think she has gotten bigger. I think he wants her to keep getting bigger so she'll have less self confidence and let him continue running over her. You know how much she runs her mouth. She said he brought her a diamond tennis bracelet. Then, in the same breath, said he got laid off from his job so she had to make the last couple of payments."

"You know we need to do two things. First, keep Christa lifted up in prayer. Second, we need to hire a private investigator to find out all about this Bryan."

"Linda, are you serious? How in God's name are we going to pull something like this off? I think we should just stay out of her business but take your first suggestion and pray. God will take care of this situation."

"You're right. I just hate for a slime ball to play our friend. Christa has a big heart and she means well. When will I get to meet this Bryan?"

"I don't know when they'll be visiting Jacksonville. I do suggest you put in a call to Christa. We need to let her know that no matter how much weight she puts on that we're still more than friends, we are sisters."

"Yes, and sisters don't let other sisters fall into a well either."

"Linda, leave it alone and let Christa find out for herself. It really might not be as bad as we think."

"Hey, you're the one who said Christa was spending her money on their meals and now she has to help pay for her own diamond bracelet. Okay, let's talk about something else."

"Yes, because you're getting a little upset over something that really isn't our business."

"Hold on Monica, I have another call. If I lose you, just hang up and I'll call you back later."

"Hello?"

"Linda, we left our friends early and will be at your house in about 15 minutes. I do hope you have something to snack on I'm famished."

"Okay, I'll see you in a minute."

"Monica, Monica. I guess we got disconnected."

Oh well, either Monica got tried of waiting on the other line or she just plain hung up. I can always call Monica back after I get dinner ready. Right now my main concern is having the food hot and ready to eat when Mother Liz walks in the door. After all, she said how much she is starving and will be here real soon.

Chapter Nine

Fifteen minutes came really fast because I heard a car pulling up. I walked over and looked out the bay window and saw Mother Liz walking towards the house.

"Hi Mother Liz. How was your visit?"

"It was nice. Linda what have you done with your hair? Turn around.

Winston, hurry up and come inside. You should see what Linda has done to her head. I can't believe you've cut all your hair off. Now why did you do that?"

Before I answered, I just stood in the middle of the floor with a hurt look on my face. I know she is my elder and I'm supposed to respect her, but this time she have pushed my panic button. This is my hair and if I want to cut it, so be it.

"Mother Liz, it's hot and I wanted a different look."

"Well you sure did. What did my son say about what you did?"

"What I did? You sound as if I committed a crime. I just cut my hair and Brandon likes the new style."

"I guess it looks okay. I'm just used to seeing you with long hair. By the way, what do you have around here to eat? I'd like for Winston to grab a bite before he leaves for the airport."

"There's some lasagna that Essie made."

"Now I don't just eat anybody's cooking. Is she clean?"

I was trying to keep a straight face. I took a deep breath and said to myself, 'God please, please help me with this lady.' "Mother Liz she is an excellent cook and yes, she is neat and clean."

"Then come on Winston, let's wash our hands and eat."

She must have been starving because she didn't even go in the nursery to peek at Brianna.

I told Mother Liz to go in the family room to wait for me to get the garlic toast ready. She said to come get them when the food was on the table. She wanted to help Daddy Alexander pack for his Miami golf trip.

I placed their food on the formal dining room table. I even had a nice glass of cold ice tea with lemon for Daddy Alexander and a crystal empty glass for Mother Liz. I knew she didn't want any tea and I wasn't about to pour her a glass of wine. I walked over to the intercom to call them to dinner. Mother Liz answered and said they were on their way.

I left the dining room to check on Brianna. She was awake and just lying there looking around. I fed and changed her into another outfit, so that when Brandon came home she would look like a little princess.

By the time Brianna and I got back to the dining room, they were both eating and discussing how tasty the meal was.

Daddy Alexander said, "Linda, this is the best tea I think I've ever had."

Mother Liz didn't say a word. She just held a glass of red wine to her lips.

Brianna and I left the dining room and went into the family room to wait until they finished their dinner. I wanted them to spend some quality time together.

After the meal, Daddy Alexander thanked me again and said to tell Essie that the lasagna was very good. He went to the bedroom and came back with his suitcase. He took Brianna from my arms and gave her a goodbye kiss. He hugged me and said for me to take care of Liz while he was away. I tried to smile, but I wasn't really feeling it. Brianna and I walked him to the door. I felt like a child being left at daycare for the first time. I really didn't want him to leave Mother Liz with me. Again I tried to smile but I couldn't when my heart was saying, "Take her with you, PLEASE!"

I left Mother Liz standing outside saying her goodbyes to Daddy Alexander. I went back into the family room not to watch TV, but to call Monica to apologize for our last conversation.

Just as I reached for the phone to call Monica, the guard from our guard station called.

"Mrs. Alexander, are you expecting a guest?"

"No."

"There is a lady here by the name of Dr. Olivia Wadsworth to see you."

Just as I was about to answer, Mother Liz had made it back in and heard the name.

"Olivia, yes, please let her in."

"Linda, this is the reason I came back so fast. Olivia is here for a conference. I told her to please come by to see Brandon and of course, you and Brianna."

"Mother Liz, why didn't you tell me she was in town

when you first came in?"

"I was hungry and I really thought she was coming by a little later."

"You let her in. I'm going to freshen up. I don't want to meet her for the first time looking like this."

"Oh Linda, Olivia is family, you don't have to change."

"Yes I do. I'll leave Brianna in here with you."

I rushed off to get myself together. There was no way was I going to meet the lady who mother Liz wanted Brandon to marry to see me like this. I put on a nice pantsuit, combed my hair and freshened up my makeup.

I must have tried on three or four outfits and nothing seemed to fit. Then I tried on a black Jones of New York. This was one of the outfits I bought during my pregnancy, so there should have been plenty of room in it. I zipped up the pants and almost laughed out loud because there was room. I walked over to the full length mirror to take one last look before making my grand entrance. I must have been in there a little longer than I intended because intercom buzzed.

"Linda, honey, how long will you be? You do have company."

I walked over to answer. I really wanted to say 'No, you have company. I never invited her to our home'. "Just a moment Mother Liz, I'm on my way. Please tell Olivia to make herself comfortable."

I made it to the family room with shaking knees and a nervous stomach. I tried to put on a friendly smile to make Olivia feel welcome, but I couldn't. I was standing before the lady who could have easily been my husband's wife. I didn't know what to do or say. I just stood looking at this beautiful petite, pecan-brown skinned lady, with flowing thick black shoulder length hair. The length I used to have before cutting it.

She walked over and flashed those pearly white teeth. I extended my hand to welcome her. Her hand was as soft as the skin looked on her flawless face.

"I'm Olivia and I've heard so many nice things about you."

While shaking her hand, my eyes looked at her French manicured nail and no wedding ring on the left hand.

"Do take a seat. Can I get you anything?"

"No, I just ate. I would like to use your bathroom if that's okay."

Just as I was about to show her where one was, Mother Liz chimed in. "Olivia you don't have to ask to use the bathroom. This is my son's house. I'll show you where one is and then I'll show you the house."

I just moved aside to let Mother Liz have her way. As soon as they left the room, I can feel the tears welling up in my eyes. I knew if I blinked they would start running down my face. I wiped the tears and just shook my head from side to side. I was standing in my own home feeling like an outsider. Mother Liz had a way of making me feel small. I just felt like screaming at the top of my lungs, "Get Out!"

Finally they came back to the family room. Olivia said, "Your home is beautiful. It looks like it should be showcased in a magazine."

I thanked her for the compliment while reaching down to pick up Brianna. Olivia asked if she could hold her. She knew this was my first baby because she said, "I know how new mothers are, so I've washed my hands."

I passed Brianna over to her. She was quite gentle with her. She kept talking to Brianna while Mother Liz and I looked at them.

I heard noise in the garage, then the door opened. It was Brandon.

As he was getting close to the family room, he said, "Hey, whose car is that outside?"

He entered into the family room where we were all sitting around. He stopped, looked and smiled. His eyes were big as tennis balls. He said, "Olivia, is that you? What are you doing in Georgia?"

She walked over with Brianna in one hand and gave him a hug with the other. She said, "I'm here attending a conference for a few days. Your mother and I keep in touch and I told her I would be down here the same time they were. She called me this morning and invited me to come out to surprise you and meet your lovely wife in person since I wasn't able to attend your wedding."

"Brandon, you have a beautiful family and Brianna looks just like you."

"Thank you. What does your schedule look like? I would like to grill out and have you over for a meal. Did Linda take you on the tour of the house?"

"No, your mother beat her to it."

"Did you see the backyard?"

"No, just the inside and it's beautiful."

"Linda, take Brianna from Olivia while I take her to see the backyard."

"Okay, come on Brianna. It's your feeding time anyway."

I reached over to take her from Olivia when she said, "Linda, you do have a beautiful baby and your home is just lovely.

I thanked her and watched Brandon eagerly take her to show off the backyard. Mother Liz looked at me and flashed a big smile while lifting her glass of wine to her lips.

I just turned my head toward the blank TV screen. My thoughts were that Brandon usually comes in with a smile and a kiss for us, but when he walked into the family room and laid eyes on Olivia, he remembered the smile, but forgot about the kiss for Brianna and me.

Chapter Ten

I got up early, took my shower and spent some quality time in the nursery reading some of my favorite scriptures, since Brandon was gone and Mother Liz and Brianna were still sleeping. Leaving the nursery I walked outside to get some fresh air and call Mom.

"Good morning, Mom, did I wake you?"

"No, I'm up early because I couldn't sleep."

"Couldn't sleep? Are you okay?"

"Yes, sometimes I have restless nights, but I'm all right."

"I'm calling because Brandon will be having a BBQ tomorrow, so please tell Dad to make sure he comes over to spend the last evening with Brandon's parents and enjoy the good food."

"How did my grandbaby sleep last night?"

"She did well, but I didn't sleep too well."

"Why?"

"Mom, Mother Liz invited Olivia to our home yesterday without asking us."

"Honey, I remember you telling me about her. This is the woman who Mother Liz wanted Brandon to marry. Remember, they're just childhood friends. Please don't let your emotions get the best of you."

"Mom it's easy for you to say, you're not here with her. Ever since Olivia came to town, her name is all that comes out of Mother Liz's mouth."

"Linda, you know the Lord and you know Satan. Don't let this get you all upset. Brandon loves you very much. Another thing, you only have to put up with Lady Liz for one more day!"

"Mom, you're right. I'm just staying prayerful that God will take care of it all."

"You said Brandon will be grilling. I'll prepare some vegetables, deviled eggs, salads, and desserts."

"Mom, you don't have to go to all that trouble. I'll fix something to go along with the meat."

"Linda, you know I'm willing to help out. You just rest. I really don't have any plans today so this will be good for me. Maybe I'll even pick some greens and cook them."

"Mom you'll be all tuckered out doing all of this."

"Good! Maybe I'll sleep well tonight. What plans do you have with Liz today?"

"None! She and Olivia are spending most of the day together. Olivia was nice enough to invite me, but I declined. I'm just going to stay around the house. Essie will be coming over because she has another engagement this week. I'll probably get her to bake one of her delicious apple cobblers."

"I sure hope so because they are delicious. Honey, I'm getting off the phone, but I do want you to know that God is your source of strength. He is the only one who can keep you when you are feeling down. Stay prayerful and keep your chin up."

"Thanks, Mom."

I went back into the house and walked into the nursery to check on Brianna. She was still sleeping. I turned on the intercom so that if she did wake I could hear her. I walked into the kitchen to start breakfast as Essie was quietly tipping in.

"Good morning, Linda. I was trying to be quiet just in case you and your in-laws were sleeping late this beautiful morning."

"Good morning, Essie Mother Liz and I are the only ones here. Daddy Alexander is in Miami and will not be back until tomorrow. Oh, speaking of tomorrow, Brandon will be grilling out. Would you and your family like to come over?"

"I wish we could, but we have plans. Thanks for the offer, though."

"I do need a favor of you."

"Anything, just ask."

"If I give you some money, would you go to the store and bring back everything you need to make a nice size pan of apple cobbler."

"Linda, is that the only dessert you want? If not, I can make a 7-up pound cake, too."

"Mom said she will be bringing some desserts, so just the cobbler and some ice cream will be enough. By the way, my in-laws really did enjoy your lasagna, especially Daddy Alexander."

"Linda, you go on with that. I hate that I told you about him looking handsome like my deceased husband. Now you've got me blushing all over myself. You don't have to go to the bedroom looking for your purse. I'll bring the receipt back. Then you can just write me a check. See you in a little while."

I didn't want a heavy breakfast and was hoping neither would Mother Liz. I thought fresh fruit, pan sausage and bagels and cream cheese would do.

I finished breakfast when I heard Brianna crying. I walked into the nursery and there she was in her crib fussing. I picked her up to change and feed her.

"Good morning, Linda. I thought I heard Brianna crying."

"Oh Mother Liz, did she disturb you?"

"No, by now I should have been up. I sure hope you don't go to all the trouble of making breakfast. I feel like a cup of coffee and a sweet roll this morning."

"I have some fresh fruit, pan sausage, bagels and cream cheese. I could call Essie on her cell phone and have her to pick up some sweet rolls from the bakery."

"No, what you have is good enough. You go on and nurse Brianna. I'll head to the kitchen for breakfast."

I got Brianna all taken care of and walked back into the kitchen to make myself a small plate. Essie was back with the groceries and had started making the cobbler.

"Essie, where is Mother Liz?"

"She got some breakfast and a cup of coffee and went out back. She said she wanted to take in the fresh air."

"Okay, I'll probably go out there and join her."

"I don't know if that's a good idea. She's been on her cell phone and I couldn't make out what she was saying, but a few times she got loud with whomever she's talking with."

"Maybe you're right. I think I'll just stay in here with you, Essie. After I eat I'll write you a check for this and a little more for all your troubles."

"Now Linda, you or Brandon have never been a problem. If I didn't want to do this I never would have agreed. Please only pay me for what's on the receipt."

"Thanks, Essie, for everything."

"You're welcome. I just wish I could be here tomorrow to be with you."

"Do you want me to freeze some cobbler for you?"

"No, I can make a cobbler anytime for me and my family. You all just enjoy."

Mother Liz came back and the look on her face told that she wasn't as happy as when she first got up this morning.

I felt like I was stepping out on an edge of a cliff by saying, "Mother Liz is everything all right?"

"Yes. I'm going to lie down for a little while before Olivia arrives."

"What time do you want me to wake you?"

"Don't bother. I won't be sleeping that hard. I'll be up soon, but thanks."

I just stood there watching as she slowly walked down the hall to the guest room. The expression on her face was one of someone who had some heavy burdens on her mind.

I took Brianna and went into my office to answer some emails. I logged in and saw there were several work related emails and one from Monica and Christa. I read over Monica's email and nothing was mentioned about Christa and Bryan, so I skipped down to see what Christa had to say. Christa said she was making plans to visit me next month. She also said she wished Bryan could come so we could meet him, but just she and Monica were coming this time. As I was about to answer her, I heard a voice calling my name. "Linda, honey, I'm up and will be getting dressed for my day with Olivia."

I turned around and she was standing in my doorway with a guilty look on her face. She looked down at Brianna. She picked her up and said, "Linda, are you sure you don't want to pal around with us today?"

"No. But thanks for the offer."

She played with Brianna a little more, then put her back in her carrier and said she was going to get dressed before Olivia arrived.

Chapter Eleven

I decided to take a little break from the computer. Brianna was no trouble at all, but I knew by now she would be getting tired and hungry. I picked her up and yes, she was ready to be changed.

As I finished feeding her and putting her in her crib, Mother Liz walked in dressed in a white short sleeved designer pantsuit. She was sporting all the family jewels like her diamond necklace, diamond earrings, and diamond tennis bracelet. She's a classic looking lady with her mixed gray and black hair worn off her round face.

"Mother Liz, you look very nice."

"Why thank you, my dear. I'll be waiting in the family room for Olivia. Are you very sure you don't want to be with us?"

"Yes, I have some work to do, but thanks again."

I went back into my office to do some computer work. I was working away, when I thought I heard noise from the baby monitor. I stopped to listen. Then she let out two short cries. I listened again, but this time there were no more sounds. Brianna must have had a little nightmare. I had turned my attention back to entering numbers when I thought I felt someone looking over my shoulder. I turned and it was Mother Liz standing in the doorway. I just looked at her for a moment. I then said, "Mother Liz is there anything wrong?"

"No. I came to tell you that Olivia is outside waiting. I'll lock the door behind me."

"Okay. I'll see you later."

That was odd, she sneaking up on me. Surely she didn't think I was in here chatting online with some strange man. Speaking of strange actions, she has asked me twice to go with them. I think I'll call Lynda to see what's up with Mother Liz.

I saved my document because I didn't want to lose all the numbers that I had just entered. Walking back into the nursery, I looked in on Brianna, came back and went to call Lynda.

Brianna was still sleeping, so I went into the kitchen to get a glass of cold ice tea, and called Lynda.

"Lynda, this is Linda, how are things going?"

"I need to ask you that question! You're the one who is dealing with Mother. She called me and told me that Olivia was there and I let her have it big time. Brandon and my father treat Olivia like a member of our family, and Mother always wanted Olivia for her daughter-in-law. I told her that I didn't like it one bit, she started yelling at me and I ended the conversation by hanging up on her."

"My maid, Essie, said Mother Liz was yelling in the phone at someone. Now I know that person was you. It's okay that Olivia is here. She seems to be very nice and Brandon was happy when he saw her."

"Yes, but don't let Mom make you feel uncomfortable in

your own home. She has a way of making people feel like they are beneath her. She kills me walking around like a queen bee."

"No. Not a queen bee, but royalty. Hi, I'm "Lady Liz.""

We both started laughing. Lynda said, "Enough about her. I had to deal with her all my life. If you don't mind I would like to change the subject and let you know what has been happening with me in this economy."

Lynda and I talked and laughed some more. I ended the conversation by telling her that as soon as Brianna turned six months we were thinking of flying to Chicago for a long weekend visit.

The conversation with Lynda, put me in the mood to call Monica and Christa. I logged off of the computer and picked up the phone to call Monica first. I dialed her number and got voice mail. I left a message that I was returning her call and hung up.

I dialed Christa and she answered on the second ring. "Hi Christa, this is Linda, how are things going?"

"Life is good and I'm happy. I want to come and see my little niece but really can't get Monica to commit to a date."

"Why don't you two set the date, then call me on three way and we'll make plans. Now tell me all about this mystery man named Bryan."

"Oh I see Monica has been running her mouth. I'll email you a picture of us on the beach. He is so handsome and has long dreadlocks. I feel like I'm dating a native from Jamaica."

"Girl, you are so happy. I can hear the happiness in your voice. Tell me more."

"Like what? I told you he makes me happy. That's all you

need to know."

"I've been out the loop of things so why don't you bring me up-to-date. Now tell me all about Mr. Bryan or does he have a last name."

"Okay, I met Bryan Whitaker online. Now before you say anything. Monica and her husband have been out with us and Monica thinks he's nice."

"What do you know about Mr. Whitaker? Is there a former Mrs. Whitaker? Are there any children involved with this man? Who are his parents?"

"Wait a minute! Are you investigating my man?"

"No! You're like a sister to me and I just don't want you hurt."

"Linda, do you think I would be stupid enough to let someone hurt me?"

I didn't answer right away. I was holding the phone thinking, this is the man who talked you into moving to Orlando leaving all your family and friends. This is the man who has made you pay his way whenever you are out on a so-called-date.

I cleared my throat and said, "Christa I guess you're old enough to know when someone is in love with you or using you."

"Well, you can stop talking like that because Bryan loves me."

"Where does this Bryan Whitaker works?"

"He's in between jobs just now. You know, this economy is causing a lot of people to get laid off, but he's looking every day."

"I understand completely. You seem to be happy and I guess that's all that matters."

"Now you're talking my language. Like I said, he is so nice to me. I can't wait for you to meet him. I'm going to my computer to scan the picture and send it to you right now. I'll also talk with Monica and we'll set a date to come up to see Brianna real soon."

"Okay, it's been good talking with you. Please take care of yourself and I'm looking forward to seeing this picture of you and Bryan. Take care and may God continue to bless you."

"Love you and kiss Brianna for me."

"I will. Bye for now."

I couldn't hang up the phone quick enough. I couldn't believe my ears! Christa was not a dumb woman and she has book smarts.

I turned the computer on to email Monica, when I got a "you've got mail" message. I clicked and it was a picture of Christa and Bryan. She was really in a hurry to get this picture to me. They were standing on the beach. Christa was wearing an orange and black flowered sleeveless dress. I could really see her weight gain in this picture. Bryan was standing next to her with his arm around her shoulders. He was a tall, brown skinned, thin man with beautiful white teeth. His hair was worn in shoulder length dreadlocks. He even had on a pair of designer sunglasses so I couldn't see his eyes. My first thought was that he was hiding behind those sunglasses or maybe he wanted to look cool for the picture.

Christa was all smiles. I could tell by the look on her face that she really liked the attention he gave her. I guess with Monica and me being married, she wants someone to love too. My thoughts are, "Why him?" He doesn't even work. How could he support her without a job? I guess these are questions that she's not asking herself. Christa is happy and I should be too!

Chapter Twelve

For three weeks I have avoided talking to Mother Liz. When I think about how she treated me at the BBQ in my own backyard, I get sick to my stomach. She kept talking about the things that Brandon and Olivia used to do while growing up. From the expressions on Olivia's face, I could tell she hated how Mother Liz kept trying to belittle me.

Mom told me that if I stayed angry with Mother Liz, then she won and Mom was right. Mother Liz knows that I'm angry because she conveniently calls in the evening when Brandon is home and never asks to speak with me. Today, I'm going to take that advice I gave my hair stylist, Marilyn: Don't let anyone take your joy. I'm going to be the bigger of the two of us and call her!

First, I'd better pray and ask God to please direct my tongue and let her have a receiving heart to accept what I'm about to say.

I started dialing the number, when I said to myself, "What am I going to say? Holy Spirit, please speak through me."

Oh my goodness my hands are actually shaking. I hope Daddy Alexander answers. Then I don't have to talk to her.

"Hello, Mother Liz, this is Linda. How are you?"

"Oh. Linda, what a pleasant surprise! How are Brandon and Brianna?"

"They are doing well by the grace of God. Brianna is growing like a weed and smiling a lot. She's coming into her own little personality. Most of all, she's sleeping longer."

"Winston and I are doing great. We are making plans with some friends to take a trip next month. We thought we would stay on Martha's Vineyard for a few days."

"That sounds like fun. I think when Brianna gets a little older, Brandon and I are going to leave her with my parents and take a short vacation."

"Do you have a location in mind?"

"No, not yet. I hope to visit my friends in Florida."

"That would be nice. Would you like to speak with Winston?"

"No. Please tell him I called. I really want to talk to you." Lord, please give me the words to say. "Mother Liz, I think you owe me an apology."

"Apology! For what?"

"First of all, I'm not dating Brandon. I'm his wife. I personally feel you should have consulted us before inviting Olivia to our home."

"I didn't feel I needed to ask permission for an old friend to visit with my son at his house!"

"That's another thing. This house belongs to us. I sold my condo and with the proceeds I made a large down payment on this house. And, Brandon works hard and makes a very nice salary and so do I. For the record, you're looking at a six-figure lady. I really didn't want it to come to this, but you have always treated me like I wasn't good enough for your son."

"I never treated you like that. And if I made you feel unwelcome in your own home, then please forgive me. I don't want to do anything to cause problems between you and Brandon."

"Well, if you honestly feel this way, then I accept your apology."

"Linda, this is Daddy Alexander. What has Liz done now? I came in at the tail end of your conversation. All I heard was her apologizing."

"Daddy Alexander, I know it has been three weeks since you and Mother Liz were here. I have pondered over saying anything about Olivia's visit."

"Honey, I didn't know she was coming to Georgia, so it was news to me."

"From the time she came into our home. Mother Liz started treating me like I was less than a desirable in my own home. She was the one who invited Olivia to the BBQ and you saw how she kept bringing up old memories. I feel she just disrespected me all together."

"I told her how I didn't appreciate how she acted in your presence with Olivia. I also told her, that she owed you an apology and for her to call you, but I guess she didn't. Like I said, I didn't like that one bit. You're Brandon's wife and I personally feel that he chose the right wife. You're a good mother, good wife, and a God–fearing lady. I'm proud to call you my daughter-in-law."

"Thank you Daddy Alexander. You have made this call worth it. Please do me a favor and don't tell Brandon about this. I don't want him to have any senseless worries."

"I won't. And again, thank you for clearing the air. I can assure you from this day forward, all of this nonsense is behind us. We both love you and are happy you're in the family."

"Thank you so much. Now have a good day."

"Before you hang up, please be sure to kiss Brianna for us."

"I will. Bye for now."

"Bye."

Daddy Alexander's words kept ringing in my ear, that things would be different. I pray he isn't just talking, but will have another talk with Mother Liz, so that things will be different. All I ever wanted was for her to accept me and love me as her daughter-in-law.

"Lord, please change her heart toward me."

I spent the rest of the day feeling pretty good. While Brianna was still sleeping, I called mom to see if she would keep the baby for a few hours.

"Hi Mom, how are you?"

"Hi Linda, what's up?"

"If you aren't busy, I would like to call Marilyn to get my hair washed and set. I would also like to sit around the shop and have a little 'me' time with the ladies."

"I'm free, so bring her over. You deserve to get out and enjoy your day."

"Thanks. I'll see you in a little while."

I couldn't hang up fast enough. It would be good to sit around and listen to the ladies talk about so many subjects. I sure hope Marilyn has a spot open for me.

"Hello. May I speak with Marilyn."

"Marilyn had to run an errand. May I help you with

something?"

"Is Brenda there?"

"Just a minute. I'll call her to the phone."

"Hello, this is Brenda."

"Brenda, this is Linda."

"Linda! who?"

"Brenda, stop acting crazy. This is Linda Alexander."

"Gurl, I know your voice. Marilyn, had to run to the bank, but she'll be back."

"I wanted to get my hair done today. Can I get a manicure and pedicure too?"

"How long are we talking about because there are about three ladies waiting to get their hands and feet done?"

"By the time I take Brianna to my mother's house. Then take the expressway to the shop, at least two of those ladies would be finished

"Okay, come on in. I'll sign you in."

"Are you sure Marilyn will be back today?"

"Girl, can you keep a secret?"

"Brenda, don't put Marilyn's business in the street."

"She put her own business in the street, when she started running her mouth off in this shop about her soon–to-be ex. She's at the bank closing all her accounts. He has been writing checks on one of her personal accounts. I thought she was smart enough to have closed them a while ago."

"Okay Brenda. I'll see you in a little bit. If Marilyn makes it back before I get there, please let her know that I would like a wash and set."

"Okay, but don't say a word about the bank situation."

"I won't. See you later. Bye."

"Bye."

Chapter Thirteen

Praise the Lord! Today, Brianna is five months old and I'll be returning to the office in four weeks. Brandon is leaving tomorrow for a four day conference and Monica and Christa are arriving tomorrow to spend a few days with me. This couldn't have worked out any better.

Mom said she would keep Brianna so the girls and I could really enjoy each other. I took out a tablet and started making plans for things to do while they're here. When they arrive, we'll spend time at home with Brianna, then I'll Invite Mom and Dad over for a BBQ. Afterward, Mom and Dad can take Brianna home for a couple of days.

Day two, will be a spa day at Marilyn's place, getting our manicures and pedicures, and then going next door for a full one-hour massage. After that we'll go downtown for an early dinner.

Day three, we'll do a little shopping, then lunch at one of my favorite soul food restaurants. Then we'll visit the movie store and get some movies to bring home for a movie and pizza night.

The last day, we'll go to church, then to Mom and Dad's for a meal. Afterward, they can leave in enough time to take back the rental car and make their flight on time.

"Honey, I'm home. Have you finished getting my things packed?"

"Oh, Brandon, I laid everything out on the bed and was just waiting for you to check them. I think I have everything. I'm so excited about seeing the girls I can't stand it."

"I know you have plans all laid out for them. The moment they told you they were coming you were floating on cloud nine."

"I just hate it that you won't be here to see them, but I'll tell you all about it when you come home."

"I hope you remembered this morning that I told you not to cook. We're going out for seafood."

"I remembered. After we finish packing your luggage, I'll get Brianna and me dressed for dinner. You just look these things over and make sure I didn't leave out anything before putting them in the suitcase."

After getting Brandon all ready for his trip, it was time to get Brianna dressed and the baby bag packed for dinner. I finally got myself ready and walked into the family room only to find Brandon sitting and talking on the telephone. I waved my hand to let him know to get off the phone. I was hungry. I didn't know who he was talking to until I heard him say, "I'll let her know you asked about her and yes, I'll kiss Brianna for you. Bye Mom, and I love you."

"I didn't hear the telephone ring."

"No. I just wanted to put in a call to Mom before my flight in the morning. She and Dad are doing well and send their love."

"Okay, if you get the baby and put her in the car seat, I'll grab her bag and lock up."

"Come on Brianna, Daddy is taking his girls to dinner."

He started kissing her and she smiled at him as they walked to the car.

The next morning, I turned over and Brandon wasn't in the bed beside me. I got up and went to the nursery. He was in there sitting in the rocking chair with Brianna in his arms.

"Good morning, Brandon. Why didn't you wake me?"

"You were sleeping so peacefully and I heard you during the night when you got up to feed Brianna. I was going to wake you before I left for the airport."

"Do you want a bagel and a cup of coffee?"

"No. I'll grab something at the airport."

"Okay, stay in here with her while I go and freshen up."

"Okay. I just wanted to spend a little time with her before leaving. Take your time."

After I got myself freshened up, Brianna and I walked Brandon to the car. It was already hot and I could tell it was going to be a very hot and humid day. We kissed and said our goodbyes.

Brianna and I went back into the house. I was feeling pretty good and could hardly wait for Monica and Christa to arrive this afternoon.

I made Brianna a cereal bottle, then put her in her swing, while I toasted a bagel and poured the cup of coffee I offered Brandon.

Oh, who's calling me this early in the morning? "Hello?"

"Linda, this is Monica. I'm too excited to sleep. Christa came in late yesterday and she is still asleep. Our plane will be arriving around 2:00 p.m. We are renting a car and will come straight to your house."

"I've been making plans for you. I don't know if you remembered or not, but Brandon is gone for a few days, so we girls will have the house to ourselves."

"Yes, I remembered you telling me. Do you need me to bring anything?"

"No. Just don't miss that flight! I'm so happy that you're both coming to see Brianna and to spend some time with me before I return to work."

"Girl, we all need a break from it all. Okay, I'm getting off this phone. I'll see you later. Bye."

"Bye."

I'd better call the guard station right now, so they will know that I have two guests arriving today.

I called the guard station and put their names on the guest list. I fed Brianna and ate my breakfast. The motion put Brianna to sleep. This is good. Now I can work on the baskets.

I lay Brianna down in the crib in the nursery and hurried to my room to make up the baskets that I wanted on each bed for the girls. I folded a large towel set with Dove soap and then added some Victoria Secret shower gel, mist spray, and body cream along with a nice silk robe and a box of chocolates.

I know Christa will be the first one to comment when she gets to her room and finds her basket. "Dear Lord, I pray that my friends enjoy being here with me and hope it will be like old times. Thank you."

I'd better call Mom to let her know that I'm still looking for her and Dad to come to dinner tonight. I know they would love seeing Monica and Christa.

"Hi Mom, Monica and Christa will be here around 6:00 this evening when I'll be putting some meat on the grill. Please tell Dad, so he won't stay late at the office. I don't need you to bring anything. Remember you're still taking Brianna home for a few days."

"Yes, your dad and I are so looking forward to spending time with her. Are you sure you don't want me to bring anything? I have several large bags of greens in my freezer. All I have to do is take them out."

"No. Why don't you keep them for Sunday? After we go to church we'll come by there for dinner and then they can leave from your house for the airport."

"Sound like a good plan. I'll have dinner all ready and waiting."

"Thanks, Mom. I'd better get off the phone. I have a lot to do before they arrive."

"I'm just sitting here doing nothing. Is there anything I could do to help out?"

"No. Brianna is asleep, so I can handle it, but thanks."

"Okay, I'm going to call your dad now to tell him about dinner tonight. I'll see you later."

"Bye, Mom."

"Bye."

Chapter Fourteen

"**O**h my goodness, do I hear a car? Come on Brianna, let's go outside to see if that's Monica and Christa I hear." We couldn't get outside fast enough when I heard a loud, "We're here!"

"Oh, come on in, but first let's have a group hug."

"Oh Linda, look at Brianna, she is so cute, and looks just like her dad. Oh, your hair! I can't believe you cut all your beautiful hair!"

"Okay, Christa, don't start no mess. I needed a change and you know this baby looks like both of us."

Monica took Brianna from Christa and held her arms length and said, "I think Christa is right, this baby looks just like Brandon. Now about your hair, I love it."

"Thank you! Are we going to stand out in this hot sun or can we go into the nice cool house?"

"Monica, you get the luggage, these shoes are killing my feet. Come on Linda and show me to my room."

Christa and I left Monica outside fussing about why she had to get the luggage. I showed Christa both rooms and she ran into the one closest to my room. "Linda, I'll take this room right here. Hey, what's this on the bed?"

"Give me the baby while you take a look."

Monica was struggling down the hall with two pieces of luggage. She said "Christa, here is your luggage, now put on some bedroom shoes and go out to the car and get my luggage."

"No, I'm the oldest and the heaviest, so I'm going to sit on the bed and go through my basket."

Monica just stood there looking at Christa. She said, "Hey, do I have a room and a basket?"

"Yes, follow me down the hall. I'll show you to your room."

"How did you know which room we were going to pick?"

"Monica, you know Christa. I figured she would be the first one in, so naturally I put the larger robe in her basket. I also knew she would have wanted to be in the room next to me. She always seemed to be in competition with us."

Monica started laughing and said, "I don't think so anymore. You see we have kept our weight down and she has gained a ton. And you had a baby!"

"Monica, please don't talk about her. I can imagine it's hard to get that weight off. I heard her make a joke about being the heaviest. I'm just going to act like I don't even notice her weight gain."

"You're right. It's okay that she got the first room. As long as we're together I'm happy with that. Linda, look at all this nice stuff in my basket. Thanks."

"Hey, what are you two down here talking about?"

Monica and I said it the same time "Nothing, Christa."

"Okay Linda, after we hang up our clothes, what plans do you have for us tonight?"

"Christa, I have some steaks marinating and will be

putting them on the grill soon. If you're hungry I can go up the street and bring back some chicken."

"No, that's not necessary. Do you have any fruit?"

"Christa, follow me in the kitchen and you can look in the refrigerator and get what you want."

"Linda before you leave, I just want to say your home is beautiful and well decorated."

"Thanks Monica. Brandon and I hired a decorator and I must say she did an excellent job. You go on and keep looking around, while I show Christa to the kitchen. In fact, you ladies stop acting like you haven't been here before. You're home, so act like it."

"Christa, when you finish in the kitchen, come back to see Brianna's nursery. Her room looks like it is made for a little princess."

"She is. She's Brandon and my little princess."

"You go on and show Christa to the food, while I look around. Hey Christa! If you find some mangoes or cold watermelon, come back and get me."

"I'm not waiting on you. In fact, you better go to the car and get your luggage. I'm headed for a snack and I don't mean any salad. I'm on vacation and plan to eat and enjoy myself."

"Wow, Linda! You're got plenty of everything in here. I think I'll have some chicken salad, a piece of fresh pineapple and some crackers. Hey, can I have a devilled egg?"

"Okay Christa, let's get one thing straight. Brandon isn't here and I want you to treat this house like you would in your own home. Eat and enjoy yourself."

Monica walked in and said, "I'm going to get my luggage, then I'll have some of what I see Christa taking out of the refrigerator."

"It's chicken salad. She has a large bowl of fruit, but I only want a few pieces of pineapple."

"Christa, I'll be right back, so leave it all out on the counter for me."

"I thought she only wanted a mango or some watermelon. I knew the moment she laid eyes on what I was doing, she would want some."

"Christa, it's okay. I have plenty and if we run out I'll go to the grocery to make sure we have plenty."

Monica came back with her luggage. She struggled past us going down the hall. I turned to Christa and said, "Looks like you ladies brought lots of clothes. I thought we would do a little shopping before you leave. I want to show off some of our little shops, but it looks like your luggage is heavy already."

"No. I can always roll my things up to make room for something new."

Monica returned. "I'll hang up my things later. I think I'd better get a snack before it's all gone." She threw her big eyes in the direction of Christa. Christa was looking down at her plate. I tried hard not to laugh.

"Okay, ladies while you're eating, I'm going to feed Brianna and change her diaper. If you need me, I'll be in the nursery."

Later after getting Brianna taken care of, she did what she does best, she went straight to sleep. I left her in the crib and went in to the family room where Monica and Christa were sitting.

"Hey, what's on TV?"

"You'll have to ask Christa. I just came in here. I was in

the room hanging up my clothes and eating a few pieces of candy. Did I say thank you for such a nice welcoming gift?"

"Yes, Monica, you and Christa both thanked me. Now if you want, you can come out back while I put the steaks on the grill."

Monica asked, "What about Brianna? What if she starts crying, can you hear her?"

"I'll take the monitor out there with us. Come on let's get started before Mom and Dad arrive."

Monica said, "Oh, you mean your parents will be joining us for dinner?"

"Yes, I invited them and Sunday, after church we will go to their house for a home-cooked meal before you leave for the airport."

Christa started rubbing her hands together and smacking her lips. She said, "I sure hope she fixes some of those collard greens and macaroni and cheese."

Before I could answer, Monica said, "Look at you, ready to eat. Well, you said you were on vacation, so let me hush my mouth."

Christa said, "Yes, please hush. I'm going to eat now and worry about exercising and dieting when I get back home."

"Monica, I'll get the meat and you get the ice tea and follow me."

Christa said, "I'll get the glasses and a bag of chips."

An hour later, between talking and laughing, the steaks were finally done. I was ready for Mom and Dad to arrive. Just as I took the steaks inside, Mom and Dad were driving up.

I went back outside to tell the girls that Mom and Dad

were here. I told them we could either eat on the patio or inside where it was nice and cool.

We settled on eating inside, so we all gathered in the dining room for dinner. I asked Dad if he would lead us in a word of prayer.

Dad said, "Come let's hold hands and form a circle. We'll invite the Holy Spirit into this house. Dear Heavenly Father, first of all, I would like to thank you for bringing these two young ladies here safely. I thank you for the friendship and love they have for one another. I would like to thank you for the food we are about to eat, that it would be a nourishment for our bodies. Thank you for the hands that prepared this meal. Now Father, as we leave this place, please be with us and watch over these ladies while they are here and take them back home safe. These and other blessings we ask it all in the name of Jesus. Amen!"

We all said, "Amen."

Christa was all hands. She was passing food and piling food on her plate. When her mouth wasn't full, she was doing most of the talking. I just enjoyed my steak while watching Brianna swing in the swing set. She was kicking her legs and swinging her arms.

Mom said, "I hope you girls enjoy your stay and remember you'll be coming to our house Sunday for dinner."

Christa said, "Yes, Linda told us of your invitation. I only have one request. Will you fix some collard greens and macaroni and cheese?"

All of us started laughing. Mom laughed the hardest. She stopped long enough to answer her. She said, "Yes, Christa, no way would I have you over and not have at least one of your favorite foods."

Monica, not to be outdone, said, "Ms. Vivian, you know I have a sweet tooth, so what kind of desserts will you have with the greens and macaroni and cheese?"

"Do you have something in mind?"

"I would like a chess pie."

"I guess I can whip one up. I haven't made a chess pie in ages. I'll give it my best shot. In case it doesn't come out, can I have a second choice?"

"I love apple pie too."

Okay, ladies, let's talk about something else beside food."

Christa said, "Since you want to change the subject, what are we going to do tomorrow?"

"I made plans for us to have a spa day. We'll get a pedicure, manicure, then a massage. After the massage, we can go downtown for a meal."

Christa and Monica said the plans sounded good and they were both all for it. I told them Mom and Dad were taking Brianna home tonight and would keep her until we got out of church Sunday.

We finished our meals and went in the family room to talk some more. I told them I was going to clean the kitchen and would be in a little later. Mom and Monica asked if they could help, but I told them no. I wanted them to spend some time with my parents. I knew Mom had questions about the old neighbors and friends in Jacksonville.

I could hear the laughter all the way in the kitchen. It made me smile to have my parents and my dearest friends over. I loaded the dishwasher and walked to the nursery to get Brianna's things. I had mixed emotions about her leaving for a few days. This would to be the first time she was away from me for this long.

Just as I put her last piece of clothing in the bag and was about to zip it up, I felt a hand across my shoulder.

"Mom, I didn't hear you come in."

"No, you were deep in thought. We'll take good care of Brianna."

"I know, but you have to understand, this will be the first time she's going to be away from me for this long."

"I know, but you need to have some fun with your friends and she would just be in the way. I know you'll be calling to check on her."

"Yes. Speaking of checking on someone, I haven't heard from Brandon since he left. I better call him and make sure everything is okay."

"I'll take her bags to the car. You go on and make the call."

Mom was right. I needed to check on Brandon. I went into our room and got my cell phone from my purse. As I sat down, I took a deep breath and then dialed his number. It went straight to voice mail.

"Brandon. This is Linda. I've been busy and a little concerned that I haven't heard from you. Please call to let me know that you made it to the conference. I love you. Bye."

This is silly. Let me check my voice mail to see if I've missed his call. I looked and listened and no, not a missed call from anyone. Oh my God, I pray Brandon is all right!

Chapter Fifteen

I looked at the clock and it was 10:00 a.m. I didn't want to wake my friends, so I took a quick shower and went in the kitchen to make a light breakfast.

I came out dressed for the day. I was walking down the hall when I thought I smelled something cooking. I went into the kitchen and saw Monica mixing something in a glass bowl.

"Good morning, Monica. I see you found everything you need."

"You said to make this our home, so I did. I wanted to thank you so much for having us that I got up early, made a call to my husband and then came in here to fix some breakfast."

"Oh Monica, you didn't have to do this. You're on vacation."

"I would have had to do it if I was at home."

"What are you cooking anyway? I can smell the sausage."

"I thought some pancakes, sausage, and scrambled eggs would do the trick."

I was about to thank her for breakfast, when we heard noises coming down the hall. It was Christa.

"Hey, good morning ladies, something smells delicious! I

don't want Monica to think I came here with her and then would not lift a finger to do anything. I'll set the table in the dining room and fill the glasses with orange juice. Are we having coffee? If so, then I'll put out the cups. I'll also have the cream and sugar on the table."

"Can I help do anything?"

Monica said, "Yes, go in the family room and turn on some of that music you had piping through the intercom."

Christa yelled! "No, I don't mean any harm, but I don't want to hear any gospel music this morning. I brought several of my CD's and I promise no rap. You will enjoy this mixture. You said to make ourselves at home. This is what I listen to on a Saturday morning while cleaning my place."

Monica looked at me and said, "Hey, you know Christa, let's hear what she has mixed up. She said no rap music."

"Okay, I'll put in a CD. I'm going to call my Mother to check on Brianna, so please don't have it blasting."

I left the room and went into my bedroom to call Mom to see how Brianna slept last night. It was late when they left. We played a board game, which lasted later than any of us thought it would. We were having so much fun-laughing and eating popcorn.

Mom answered the phone on the second ring. "Good morning, Mom. How's Brianna?"

"Good morning, Linda. Brianna slept so well last night. She had her cereal bottle and some water this morning. I'm in the kitchen cleaning up the breakfast dishes. Your father was supposed to be watching Brianna as she was swinging in her swing, but last time I looked, he was holding her. I'm so glad you left her with us. We are really having the time of our life with her."

"Do you and dad have any plans today?"

"Yes, we think we're going to take her to visit your grandmother. I know this would please your Dad and his Mother."

"What a good idea."

"Are the girls up?"

"Yes. Monica was the first one up and she's fixing breakfast."

"That's awfully nice of her. What is Christa doing?"

"She's setting up the dining room for us. I'm so happy they're here. I can't wait for us to have our day at the spa. Mom, Christa is standing in my doorway waving. She said the pancakes are hot and the butter is melting. I'll check back with you later today, to see how Brianna is doing."

"Okay, enjoy your day and I'll tell Dad you said hello."

"Tell grandmother I said hello, too. Bye for now."

"Bye."

Christa said, "Okay, can I turn up the sound now?"

"No! Let's have a prayer first."

"Okay, then either you or Monica pray over the food."

Monica, said, "I made the breakfast, so let me say a word of prayer."

We held hands, while Monica prayed over the food. She even prayed for their family members who were home.

After she finished, Monica and I sat down, but Christa went over to the intercom to turn up the volume. She had the nerve to do a little dance while walking back to the table. She said, "Go Michael, Go Michael, it's your birthday. I love that Billie Jean song."

Monica said, "No wonder you didn't want to pray over the food. Your mind is on that worldly music."

Christa put her fork down and said, "There isn't a thing wrong with what you call "worldly music." At least there isn't cursing in any of the lyrics. I'll bet if I looked under the table you're probably over there patting your feet to the beat of the music."

Monica said, "Okay, we're on vacation, so I'll give it a rest this time."

Christa started singing the song and eating like Monica and I weren't sitting there watching her.

The telephone rang so I excused myself to see who was calling. It was Brandon. He sounded so cheerful. I said, "Hi Baby, you sound happy this morning."

"Yes, we've been up for a while and I've attended one class already. Since we are taking a break, I thought I would use my time to call to see how you and Brianna are doing."

"She's doing great. Mom and Dad are really having a good time with her. Today, they are taking her to visit grandmother."

"Speaking of today, what plans you have for the girls?"

"We are having a spa day; then we're going downtown to get something to eat. After that, we'll probably come back here, sit around and chat like old times, then order pizza for dinner."

"Sound like you have it all planned out. I have to go- I see the people going back to the classroom. I just wanted to check on you and let you know that I love you and miss you."

"I love you too. See you when you get home. Bye."

"When you see Brianna, kiss her for me. Bye."

I went back to the dining room all smiles. It made me

feel good to hear his voice and especially the part where he said he loved and missed me.

Christa was finished eating and was sipping a cup of coffee. Monica was still eating. I wanted to say, "this is a switch. Usually, Christa is the one with food in her mouth."

Christa said, "From the look on your face that must have been Brandon."

"Yes, he was taking a break and wanted to see how Brianna and I were doing. He even asked what we had planned for today."

Monica said, "I'll take the dishes to the kitchen and load them in the dishwasher. Christa you still have to get dressed."

"I'll do that. You both are on vacation, remember."

"Christa said, "I think I'm going to call Bryan and see how he's doing?"

Monica said, "You mean you haven't talked with him since you've been here?"

"No! I tried calling him twice, but his phone goes into voice mail."

"Are you calling him on his cell or land phone?"

"He doesn't have a land phone. He isn't home that much anyway. Don't worry, he'll see that I've tried calling him and he'll call later."

She didn't wait for us to say a word about Bryan. She left the room in a hurry. I followed Monica in the kitchen, so that when she loaded the dishwasher I could start it.

One hour had passed when we were all finally dressed and ready for our spa day. I told them I would drive since I knew where we were going and for them to pull their rental car in the garage.

Christa got in the back seat, while Monica got up front. Christa said, "Are you going to put the top down on this BMW?"

I said, "If you want me to. I didn't want to blow your hair all over."

Christa said, "Blow my hair, honey! Ain't no reason to have a convertible if you aren't going to use it. I would kill for a convertible. I can see myself speeding and letting my hair blow in the wind."

Monica, said, "You got that right, you are a little heavy on the pedal. I wanted so much to tell you to slow down on our way here from the airport."

Christa started moving her head from one side to the other and said, "Oh, you don't like my driving? Then why didn't you drive? I could have just sat back and watched you try to remember where Linda lived."

"Okay ladies, we'll put the top down. We are going to a salon. If you want to get your hair styled, we could do that too."

No one said another word. Monica was just riding and looking. I looked in my rear view mirror and saw Christa had her head down and her fingers were moving fast across the key pad of her cell phone. My first thought was that she couldn't talk to Bryan, so now she's going to send him a text message.

By now you could tell she was getting a little irritated because she said, "Can I put in one of my CD's?"

I didn't want to upset her, so I said, "Why yes, pass it over and I'll put it right in."

Monica said, "How many did you bring? I thought you

left the CD back at Linda's house."

Honey, I always keep some music in my purse, just in case I don't like what's playing."

I just put the CD in and didn't say a word. I've noticed a change in Christa's personality. I don't know if Bryan has changed her, or if she has gotten a little bitter. No way would she conduct herself the way she has acted today. I'm just going to try and make her feel welcome and loved while she is staying with me.

The ride was a quiet one. No one had anything to say, so we just sat back and listened to the music while the wind blew through our hair.

I parked and told the ladies, "we're here. Our first visit will be at Marilyn's place to get our manicures and pedicures. When we are all done, then we'll go next door to have our one hour full-body massage."

We walked up the door and there was a note saying "Closed". How strange this was because I had just talked with Marilyn the other day to make this arrangement. I tried looking inside, but it was dark.

Christa was the first to say something, "Linda, are you sure you have the right place? There is a closed sign on the front door."

"I'm sure because the lady who owns this shop is a friend of mine. She does my hair and my mother's hair also."

Monica said, "When was the last time you talked with her?"

"I don't know the exact day, but she knew we were scheduled for today. Let's go to the shop next door to see if they know what's going on."

Christa said, "Yes, because standing in this heat looking at a closed door isn't normal. Apparently something has happened."

"You're right Christa. Come on, let's see. I'll ring the service bell."

A tall lady with a purple smock came to the door. She said, "May I help you ladies?"

"Yes, you may. My name is Linda Alexander and these are my two friends. We had an appointment with Marilyn today. Then we're coming here for a one hour full-body massage."

"Come on in. My name is Rebecca and I'm the owner. It's a terrible thing that happened to Marilyn."

"Marilyn? What happened to Marilyn?"

"The news wouldn't release the names of the victims until the family members were notified. The only reason I know is because the first officer on the scene is my cousin and he has been to both of our shops before."

"I don't understand! Please tell me what happened to Marilyn?"

"Honey, Marilyn is dead!"

Chapter Sixteen

"Rebecca, I'll have to take a seat. I just can't believe what you're saying. Marilyn is dead! What happened?"

"My cousin didn't go into it because he didn't want me talking until the facts are revealed. All he said was Marilyn and her husband were both found dead in their house."

"Their house? They were getting a divorce. Was this murder-suicide? When did this happen?"

"Like I said, my cousin said both bodies were found in their home. It happened late yesterday afternoon. The reason I can remember is because I was locking up for the day. When Marilyn and I are leaving, we always tell each other, so if we hear something we know it isn't right and to call the police immediately. When I went over to tell her, one of the ladies said she had to make a run and would be back later."

"I didn't hear anything on TV. Oh how could I? I haven't even had the news on."

"If you did, they didn't release the names until this morning. I'm the one who put the note on the door. Brenda, the receptionist, came in to get the sign-in sheet. She said she had to call to the customers to cancel. I guess she didn't get to you before you left home."

"No. I never received a call. I was shocked when I came here and saw the closed sign. Rebecca, this is a hard pill for me to swallow. If Christa and Monica still want their massage, I'll wait out here for them. I'm in no mood for this. I have to call my Mother."

"I understand completely. Ladies if you two still want your massage I'll be more than happy to take you now."

Monica came over and took a seat next to me. She said, "Linda, I'd rather not have a massage today. No way can I relax seeing how hurt you are."

Christa said, "That goes for me too. I think we should go to your Mother's house and tell her about Marilyn."

"Rebecca, what do I owe you? I think we'll just cancel for today."

"You don't owe me anything. I'm just sorry we met under these circumstances."

"Me too! I've visited your place before, but this is the first time meeting you."

"Honey, times are hard and I had to downsize. You know, cut staff. I had to do this in order to stay in business. Speaking of business? I don't know what's going to happen with Marilyn's place. Give me your telephone number, so we'll keep in touch."

"I'd like that very much. Who knows? You might have to combine these two shops and turn them into one large salon."

"Linda, only God knows if that's going to happen now. Again, it was nice meeting you and your two friends. I feel I'll see more of you. Bye for now."

"Bye."

Monica, Christa and I turned and started to slowly walk

towards the car. I said, "I'll call Mom when we get back in the car. If she's home we'll go by there. If not, then she and dad are visiting my grandmother and I don't want to spring this on her over the telephone."

We arrived at the car and got in and noticed immediately that since the top was up the car had gotten hot. I started the car and we sat there while the air condition ran to cool the car off. I wanted to call mom to tell her about Marilyn. I took out my cell and dialed her number. The telephone rung until voice mail picked up. I didn't leave a message. I just hung up.

Christa said, "What now?"

"Whatever you girls want to do is okay with me. Sure I'm upset about Marilyn, but I don't know her parents or if she has any sisters or brothers. All the time she has been doing my hair, we have never discussed her family members. All I know is that she doesn't have any children."

Christa said, "If she and her husband were getting a divorce why were they in the same house together?"

"Christa that's a good question! I personally feel that Marilyn didn't want the divorce and who knows? They might have been trying to patch things up. I guess we'll never know what happened."

Monica said, "Do you want to just drive downtown and look around."

"Okay."

Christa said, "We can always get out and walk around, then find some ice cream since it's so hot."

We had to laugh about that. I guess Christa was saying when all else fails you can't go wrong with ice cream.

We spent the rest of the day downtown. Afterward I

took them to my favorite restaurant for some fried catfish. Monica didn't eat all her food so she got a carry out box. I only ordered a sandwich because I wasn't hungry. Christa ordered a full dinner with a piece of lemon cake to go.

When I got home I was a little tired, but wanted to call Mom to see how Brianna's day went. I waited until the girls were in their rooms, then I went to the family room to make the call, just in case I started to cry when I got to the part about Marilyn's death.

"Hi Mom, how's Brianna doing?"

"Brianna is asleep and so is your Dad. Our visit with Mom was nice. We even stayed a little longer because they had an ice cream social. You know how your father likes ice cream. Hey, have you seen the news yet?"

"No. But I heard about Marilyn's death."

"Yes, when we got home I got a call from one of her customers. I just can't believe it. I don't really know what happened, but I think Marilyn wanted him back and didn't want to live without him."

Choking up, I was able to say, "Oh Mom, I'm just so sorry this happened to her. She really had so much to live for. Life is precious. I just wish I could have said something or done something for her."

"Linda, I feel the same way. The last time she did my hair, we talked about life and the goodness of the Lord. She didn't do much talking but she did listen to what I had to say. I even wrote down some scriptures for her to read. I just feel like I should have done more."

"Mom I better go on and try and cheer up myself. Hopefully we can sit around and eat popcorn and laugh like we used to do. Kiss Brianna for me and tell Dad I said hello."

"I'll do that, and Linda, keep your chin up and enjoy Monica and Christa. I'll see you all tomorrow after church. I love you."

"I love you, too. Bye."

Dear Lord, this is one time in my life that I just don't know what to say or how to pray. I think this is the time Mrs. Carrie used to say, "Keep the word in your heart." I remember she told me in Psalm 147:3 *God healeth the broken in heart, and bindeth up their wounds.* Lord, please bind my wounds. I'm hurting for the loss of Marilyn and I pray that she didn't kill her husband and take her own life.

"Monica, I didn't hear you come in. I had my head down saying a little prayer. I guess this thing with Marilyn has really touched me."

"I bet it has. I didn't know her, but from what little I've learned today, it's a tragedy. Just knowing that you talk with someone, make plans to see them, then they're gone. I mean like that. I do hope she didn't kill herself. Do you know if she was saved?"

"No. All I know is when I would talk to her about the Lord, she would listen. We never discussed what church she attended or even if she knew God. Like I said, she would listen, so that led me to believe she did know of God. You asked me was she saved. I can't answer that one. I pray that she was."

Christa came in the family room. "I can't believe it! I tried calling Bryan again and still no answer. He needs to call me. He forgot he has my car and will have to drive to Jacksonville to pick me up Monday. I'm staying Sunday night at my parent's house."

Monica said, "You mean all the time we've been here you haven't had contact with him once?"

"No, I didn't need to. I gave him my debit card so if he needed some gas, he could fill up my car."

"Christa, you're a full grown adult and you make your own living. But I have got to say something. Why in the world would you give him your debit card?"

"Monica, this isn't your business. Why are you asking me about my debit card?"

"Monica, don't answer. Christa, you're the one who brought up the subject that you haven't heard from Bryan. You're also the one who told us about the debit card. You can't get upset with us when you're the one being used by this man."

"Linda, this has nothing to do with you either. Neither one of you know anything about Bryan."

Monica said, "And neither do you. Christa, I've sat around long enough to see and hear this man take advantage of you. When you pulled up to my house and said he was keeping your car, I almost lost it. Are you this desperate for a companion?"

"Desperate! I know you aren't calling me desperate."

"Christa, what I think Monica is saying is, you have too much on the ball to be with a loser like Bryan."

"Linda, you don't even know him. How can you call him a loser? For your information, we are thinking about getting married soon."

"Does he have a job? How can he support you?"

"He's looking for a job."

"Christa, have you ever wondered why this man can't keep a job? Have you ever thought about doing a background check on him?"

"Why Linda Alexander! I can't believe you! Ms. Holier-Than- Thou!"

"What did you call me?"

"Perhaps I need to get in your face and say it again. I called you Ms. Holier Than Thou!"

"Christa, you are angry with Bryan because you don't know where he is. You don't know where your car is, and you probably don't have any money left in that account."

"I'll have you to know that Bryan loves me. He's probably working somewhere and doesn't want to worry me. He wants me to have a good time with my friends. Or should I say friends, loosely."

Monica said, "Come on now. Linda has just lost a friend and look at us fighting about a man none of us really know. Come on, we need to stop this right now."

"I'm not stopping nothing! All I said was I haven't heard from Bryan and now Linda wants me to run a background check on him. I trust him completely."

"Okay, since you trust him completely, why don't you go into my office and get on my computer and check your balance to see if he's taken all your money."

With flared nostrils she shouted, "You know Linda, I'm not as fortunate as you and Monica. You both are married and now you have a baby to complete your life. I don't live in a million dollar mansion and I'm not married to a doctor. You have everything and now you're shoving it down my throat. I don't care to hear anymore about Bryan. In fact, I won't because I'm going into the room to pack my things and then check into the nearest hotel. You can kiss this friendship goodbye!"

"Christa, don't do this! We have been friends too long for you to act like this. I'm so sorry that I made you feel uncomfortable in my home. For the record, it's not a million dollar house!"

"If that is supposed to make me feel any better, it doesn't. Come on Monica, you can either go with me or let Linda drive you to the airport. I'm out of here!"

She stormed down the hall to the guest room. Monica looked at me and we both burst into tears.

"Monica, you go on with her. She doesn't even know her way around here. There are several hotels on the main street. It's okay that you won't be going to my church tomorrow. I'll call Mom in the morning to let her know about this falling out. I really think she's upset with Bryan and she's taking it out on both of us."

"Linda, I know you're right, and I feel bad about us leaving like this."

"I know, and I feel bad about how Christa is hurting. I pray Bryan hasn't taken her money and disappeared. I'm going to fall down on my knees tonight and pray that God will open her eyes to see the real Bryan."

"Linda, you do just that. In the meantime I better go and gather my things before she leaves me. No telling where she'll end up."

Christa came rushing past me with her luggage and said, "You don't have to worry if I took your basket. It's on the bed."

"Christa, I bought all that for you. Again, I'm so sorry this weekend has turned into a fight. I pray that God will touch your heart so you can see it's not our friendship here that's at stake, but your relationship with Bryan."

She threw her luggage on the floor, got right in my face and pointed her finger almost to my nose and shouted "You don't know anything about Bryan and my suggestion to you is to never use his name again. And in fact, forget you ever met me!"

By this time I was standing there not knowing who this woman really was. The hurtful words and the tone she used were just not part of Christa's character. I just walked away with tears streaming down my face.

Monica was still packing, or shall I say, throwing her things into the suitcases as fast as she could. I just stood there and cleared my throat. She looked at me and saw that I was crying. She came over and gave me a big hug.

"Monica, this is just not Christa. What has happened to her?"

"I don't know, but I better rush before she comes back in to get me or drives off without me."

"Monica, please be careful, I'm not going to see you to the door. When you leave, please put the bottom lock on. I'm going into my room to pray."

Chapter Seventeen

I laid in bed praying and asking God to please touch Christa's heart. I know she isn't angry with us but with Bryan.

The ringing of the telephone made me get up to see who was calling.

"Hello?"

"Hello, Linda, this is Mom. How things are going with you and the girls?"

I tried to choke back the tears. I took a hard swallow before answering. "Mom Christa and I had words and she stormed out of here so fast."

"Words? What kind of words?"

"Christa is seeing this man she met online. She hasn't heard from him since she left Orlando. I mean Jacksonville. She let him use her car and left him with her debit card to put gas in her car."

"Linda, you are talking too fast and not making sense to me. Are you saying Christa met a man online and left her car and money with this total stranger?"

"That's what I'm saying. She got upset when I told her she doesn't know anything about Bryan. That's his name. She became defensive and stormed out of here. I told Monica to please ride with her."

"Where did they go?"

"I think to the nearest hotel."

"Linda, I just hope and pray you all can come to some kind of a solution. You have been friends far too long to let a mess like this break up your friendship."

"You're right, but she said for me to never call her again. She also went as far as saying we aren't friends anymore. Oh Mom, what have I done? I feel so terrible about all of this. I shouldn't have opened my big mouth. I'm the one who suggested that she hire a private investigator to do a background check on him."

"Linda, I think you were meddling in her affairs. Christa is an adult and if she feels that she knows him, then you should have not said a word."

"Mom you called him a total stranger yourself."

"I think he is but then I wouldn't have been on the internet looking to meet a man in the first place. She must have some confidence in him because she allowed him to keep her car and bank card."

"Mom I don't want to discuss this any further. Please tell me how Brianna is doing?"

"Okay I'll change the subject. She's doing great. Are you still coming to dinner tomorrow?"

"Yes. I hear a click, so I have another call. I'll talk to you later."

"Hello?"

"Mrs. Alexander. This is Tom and I'm one of the security guards."

"Yes. May I help you?"

"I'm off- duty and I hope you don't mind me calling. I just want you to know that the two ladies that were at your house peeled out of here and hit another car."

"Hit a car? How do you know it was the same two ladies visiting my house?"

"I was coming back from my lunch hour when this accident occurred. I got out and ran to see if anyone were hurt. I looked and saw they were the two ladies who signed in to visit with you."

"Are they hurt?"

"I just know that the two ladies were taken away by ambulance and so was the one in the other car."

"Oh my God! Thank you, I know nearest hospital. Thank you. Didn't you say your name was Tom?"

"Yes."

"Thank you, Tom, for calling."

I couldn't hang up fast enough. I better call Mom to let her know what the guard just told me.

With shaking fingers I was able to dial Mom's number. "Hello Mom. The call that interrupted us was from the security guard." I couldn't complete my sentence. I started crying so hard.

"Linda, what's the matter?"

Between the sobs and tears I finally got myself together to answer. "Mom, Christa and Monica were in a car accident!"

"What! Did anyone get hurt?"

"I don't know. I'm in the process of going to the hospital now. I know they took them to the nearest one. I'll keep you posted."

"Please do. I'll be sitting here praying and waiting for

your call."

Car accident! I know Christa drives too fast and just now she was driving fast with an attitude. I just pray she and Monica aren't seriously hurt. Oh my God, please don't let them or the people they hit die!

Just as I grabbed my purse, my telephone started to ring again. I was thinking I should get this, it might be Monica.

"Hello."

"Hi Brandon, I can't talk. I'm on my way to the hospital."

"Hospital? Is Brianna okay?"

"Brianna is doing very well, she is still with Mom. I have to get the cell phone and I'll call you right back to tell you all about it."

"Linda, please don't forget. I can hear the stress in your voice."

"I promise as soon as I get in the car I'll call you right back."

I hung up and headed straight to the car. As I was backing out the garage I reached in my purse to call Brandon and my cell phone wasn't in there. I remembered it was on my night stand. I pulled back into the garage and ran into the house to get it.

After getting the phone, I rushed back to the car, sat down and took a few deep breaths. Thinking to myself, *I'm too nervous and shaking I'm in no shape to drive and talk on the phone. I better sit here and make the call to Brandon before going to the hospital.*

I dialed Brandon. "Brandon, I'd thought I better call you before leaving the house. I need to have my mind on the road and not the conversation with you. Christa met a guy online.

She left her car and debit card with him. He hasn't called her since she has been here visiting. She got upset because I told her she shouldn't have done that. I went as far as to tell her that she should run a background check on him. This really put gasoline on the fire. She started yelling, gathered her things and left. I asked Monica to ride with her. They were going to a hotel for the night, when Christa, who drives fast anyway, struck another car. I got a call from one of our security guards and now I'm on my way to the hospital to see if they are hurt."

"Oh, Baby, I'm so sorry I'm not there to be with you. Do you want me to come home now?"

"No. I'm going to check on things. Hopefully, when you return home all of this will be resolved. Thank you for calling. I feel a little better now. I love you."

"Linda, I love you too. I'll keep all of you in my prayers and when you see Brianna, please kiss her for me. Take care, Bye."

"Bye."

It was good talking to Brandon. I wiped my eyes and was ready to pull out of this garage to make my way to the hospital.

When I got to the hospital, I pulled into the emergency parking lot. I rushed in looking to see if either was still sitting in the waiting room. I walked in looking so puzzled and saw a receptionist looking in my direction.

She said, "May I help you?"

"Yes, two of my friends just came in an ambulance and I want to go back to see them."

She said there have been several ambulances that have

come in the last hour. She then asked me to write down their full names while she checked the computer. I stood there so nervous I could hardly write their names. She looked at me and told me to please have a seat.

I went and sat as close to her desk as I could. I wanted to hear the conversation just in case she had to make a call about Christa and Monica.

Finally, she waved for me to come back to the desk.

I got up and rushed to her and said, "Yes, did you find out anything?"

She said, "Yes. Both ladies are being checked for their injuries and no one can go back there at this time."

"Can you tell me if they are conscious?"

"I think I'd better let the doctor tell you everything."

"Thank you."

I went back to my seat to sit and quietly pray for their well being. I took out my small Bible and started reading Hebrews 12:1-2. *Seeing we also are compassed about with so great a cloud of witnesses, let us lay aside every weight, and the sin which doth so easily beset us, and let us run with patience the race that is set before us, looking unto Jesus the author and finisher of our faith.*

"Miss, please come here a minute."

I looked up to see if the receptionist was talking to me or someone else in the waiting room. She was pointing in my direction. I said. "Are you talking to me?"

She said, "Yes."

I closed my Bible and rushed to the desk. I said, "Have you found out anything on my two friends?"

She said, "Is your name Linda?"

"Yes."

"Then Monica is asking for you to come back. She's in room 28. When I press this button, the large two doors will open, you are to walk through them and make an immediate left turn. The room is almost to the end of the hall."

"What about my other friend Christa?"

She said, "I can't say. All I know is Monica is asking for you."

"Thank you." I wanted to tell her this confidentiality stuff has got to go.

I walked over and just stood in the front of the two large doors and waited for her to press the button. When they flew open, I found myself standing there not being able to move. My knees started to shake. I had to get my composure and said to myself, "*Lord we can do this. I don't know what I'm going to see when I reach Monica. Whatever please, please help me to face her with a positive look on my face. Amen.*"

Slowly walking down the hall, I find myself looking in every room. I was not being nosy, but hoping that I'd see Christa in one of these rooms.

I made it to room 28, when a nurse ran pass me saying, "Code Blue." The first thing I thought of was, is she talking about Christa. I rushed into the room and there was Monica. She had a bandage across her neck.

I rushed to her waiting arms. I held her while we both cried.

"Monica, I'm so sorry. This is my fault. I should have never made Christa so upset and the fact that she got behind the wheel angry was a mistake."

"Linda all you knew when we left your house was that

Christa was upset. You didn't know she would have been driving like a maniac. I didn't know she was crying and trying to dial Bryan at the same time. I looked over at her and was about to tell her to slow down when all of a sudden a car came from out of nowhere. We plowed right into them."

"Is Christa okay? Did the other person get hurt?

"I don't know about Christa or the other person. The doctors won't tell me anything. I don't even know what room Christa's in."

"Are you okay?"

"I'm just bruised and aching from the impact. I think Christa got the worse part. If I can remember, I think that air-bag hit her so hard, it knocked her out. I was sitting back far enough that it didn't harm me. I was cut when my seatbelt came across my neck and tightened up."

"I think I'm going to walk down the hall and see if I see Christa on the other side. As I was coming to visit you, I didn't see her on this hall."

"Linda, she is so upset with you. Do you think it's a good idea for her to see you?"

"I'll try to peek in and hopefully, when I locate her, she'll be asleep."

"Linda, be careful and come back and let me know something."

"I will."

I walked slowly down the other hall looking in each room. I finally came upon room 10. I looked in and there was Christa. She had a bandage on her forehead. Her left arm was in a cast and she looked as if she was asleep.

Just as I was about to walk in her room, I felt something

pulling me by my right arm. I turned and it was what looked like the tallest female nurse I've ever seen. She said, "May I help you?"

I looked up at her and wanted to say 'as soon as you let me go I'll answer you'. Instead I said, "I'm Linda Alexander, and she's my friend. May I visit with her?"

Before she could answer, we both heard noise and it was coming from Christa's room.

Christa must have heard my voice because she started shouting, "No! Don't let her near me!"

The nurse left my side to quiet her down. Another nurse came toward me and said, "This is the emergency room and you are disturbing our patient. I strongly suggest you leave immediately."

I said, "But this is my friend and I need to see her."

The nurse started escorting me to the exit doors. She said, "I don't know what kind of trick you're playing but either you leave with me or I'll have security throw you out!"

While walking with her I kept trying to explain that we were friends and that I really needed to talk with her. The nurse didn't say another word, as she walked me to the exit doors.

Chapter Eighteen

I went back in the emergency waiting room. I waited and waited. Finally, a man came in and the nurse pressed the button for him to enter. I rushed behind him and headed towards Monica's room feeling awful bad. Christa's shouting words will haunt me for a long time. Lord, I'm so sorry that I caused my two best friends to end up in the hospital. How could I ever make up with them and how could they ever forgive me.

Monica was lying there with her eyes closed. I said, "Monica, I got to see Christa."

She opened her eyes and turned to look at me and said, "Is she okay?"

"I think she is. I saw some bandages on her forehead and what look like a cast on her left or right arm. She shouted for me to leave and the nurse escorted me right out. I really hope she doesn't come back through this hall and find me in here with you."

"Linda, I'm so sorry all of this has happened. It really wasn't your fault. Christa is really angry with Bryan and taking it out on you."

"I just want to apologize to her; then I'll leave. Do you

want me to wait around to see if both of you need a ride back to the hotel?"

"I think you better go on home. I'll call a car rental company and get us a car."

"Do you think you will be coming to my church tomorrow?"

"I don't know. I better wait to see if Christa will be discharged tonight. The doctor said I will."

"Okay. I won't pressure you, but if she isn't discharged you're more than welcome to stay with me."

"I know. I'll wait around to see about Christa. If she has to stay, then I'll call you and we can take care of getting our things out of the rental car. You go on home and wait for me."

"Okay, Monica. Give me a hug and I'll talk with you later."

As I walked away, the tears started to flow down my face again! All I could think of was how my two best friends, who came to visit with me, have ended up in the hospital and I can't do a thing about it.

I went back into the waiting room to call Mom. I needed to hear her sympathetic voice. After the conversation with Mom, I was ready to drive home and wait for Monica to call me.

When I arrived home it was late, but I wasn't about to go to bed, not while I was waiting to hear from Monica. I went into the kitchen got a bottle of water and a bag of butter cookies. I walked back into the family room, turned on the TV and waited for her call.

I must have fallen asleep because I was awake by the ringing of the telephone. I looked at the Caller ID, it was Monica.

"Hello, Monica, is everything okay?"

"Yes, I'm being discharged. I know it's late, but do you mind coming to get me?"

"Don't be silly, we're still friends. Are they going to discharge Christa?"

"Not tonight. The doctor said she has a concussion and they would like to watch her overnight. He said he was sure she would be discharged some time tomorrow."

"I'm on my way."

"Linda, the policeman gave me the tow company's business card. I called to see about our luggage. The man said they are open for 24- hours. I know it's late, but do you mind taking me to get our luggage?"

"Not at all. If you want, I can take you to the car rental at the airport, they are open all night. You can get another rental and turn in an accident claim."

"Linda, I just want to go to sleep. I called my husband. He wanted to drive up in the morning to take us back to Jacksonville. I told him no, we should be able to fly out like we planned. This is just like a bad dream. I'm so sorry all of this has happened. And Linda, by no means am I saying this is your fault. We both know who has caused all of this. My main concern is that Christa finds out that Bryan isn't who she thinks he is and she still has a car and money in her bank account."

"I feel the same way. Now I'm on my way to get you, so look for me. I'll be sitting in the car at the emergency entrance waiting for you come out."

I arrived at the emergency entrance looking for Monica, but she was no where to be found. Just as I was about to cut off the engine and run in to get her, I saw her through the large glass doors. The nurse was pushing her out in a wheelchair.

"Monica, are you okay?"

"Yes, I sat in a wheelchair near the door and when I saw you, I was telling the nurse who has been keeping my company that you were out there. She was kind enough to push me to the car. Now, to answer your question I'm okay, just a little tired and sore."

"Monica, I know it's late, but do you want something to eat?"

"No, I just want to get our luggage and head to your house. We can go to the car rental place in the morning. If they discharge Christa, she has my cell phone and can reach me on it."

"Monica, before we pull off, I just have to say, I didn't plan for all of this to happen. I just wanted us to have a good time together. Please forgive me."

"Linda, forgive you? You didn't cause this. You had made so many plans for us and it just turned out the way it did. I really don't want to blame Christa. Like I said before, we both know it's Bryan who has caused all of this mess. Come on let's get out of here before I get mad all over again."

Chapter Nineteen

Good Morning Holy Spirit. Today the sun is shining bright and I can't help but think that today is going to be a beautiful day in the Lord. I'm going to take a hot shower, call Mom to check on Brianna, and make some breakfast for Monica.

After the nice hot shower, I did just what I planned on doing. I called Mom to get a report on Brianna. I was about to go into the kitchen when I got a call from Brandon. He wanted to remind me that he was coming home this evening and since I had such a weekend, he would take a cab home.

While walking down the hall on my way to the kitchen, I heard a soft song coming from one of the spare bedrooms. It was Monica singing Amazing Grace. I stood outside the door to listen. She always had a beautiful voice. The words just touched my heart. I found myself wiping the tears from my eyes.

The door flew open! "Hey, are you spying on me?"

"No, just listening to your singing, you sound so good."

"I'm just giving God all the praise that we weren't killed yesterday."

"Did you ever hear anything about the person in the other

car?"

"It was just one teenager and she wasn't hurt. She was taken to the hospital to be checked out. I got this information from that nice nurse who helped me to the car."

"Speaking of car, do you want some breakfast? Then I'll take you to the car rental place at the airport."

"I can't eat a thing, I just want to make this claim, get another car, and go over to the hospital to see if Christa will be discharged."

"Let me bring in the newspaper, get my purse and I'll meet you at the back door."

I got the paper and wanted to see if there was anything in there about Marilyn's death. While flipping and running my eyes over the articles, I immediately saw the words suicide. I took a seat to read. The article said that Marilyn shot her husband, then took her own life! My God, I can't believe what I'm reading.

"Linda, the look on your face! What's the matter?"

"I was just reading this article on Marilyn. She did kill her husband and took her own life. I knew she didn't want the divorce, but I didn't think she would go out like this."

"Just when you think you know someone, you really don't. Go on and get your purse so we can get this behind us."

"What are you going to do after you pick up Christa? Your plane doesn't leave until late afternoon."

"I'll have to leave that up to her. She might want to go to the airport to see if we can get on an earlier flight. I'll call you and let you know where we are."

"I know she won't be interested in coming to my house or Mom's. You don't have to call me. I don't want her to catch you talking with me. Just call me when you get home and settled in for the night."

I got my purse and was ready to walk out, when Monica's cell phone stared ringing. She looked at me and I looked at her. Sure enough, it was Christa calling.

I stood there listening. I actually found myself holding my breath, as if she was going to see me standing there.

"Okay, I'm on my way to get a rental. I'll be there to pick you up. Are you sure you can stay there until I come to get you? Okay, then I'll call your cell when I'm close to the hospital."

"They are discharging her and she was told it was okay for her to fly back to Jacksonville. She also said, she has to have a follow-up visit with her primary physician. For some reason she sound a little cheerful. Maybe she got to talk with Mr. Bryan."

"All I know is, I'm going to take you to get this car, come back home and get myself together to meet Brandon when he comes home. We sure do have a lot to talk about."

The ride to the rental company was a quiet one. I put on my gospel tape and we listened to the sermon all the way to the airport.

Monica and I went into the office to make an accident claim and the lady behind the counter seemed as if she was having a bad morning.

Monica said, "Good morning, I have all my paperwork and would like to file a claim. The car was in an accident and I or shall I say, we, took out insurance."

The lady looked over the paperwork, looked at me, then back at Monica and said, "Where is the car?"

Monica said, "I have a card for the towing company. The car is on their lot."

She said, "You mean the car isn't drivable?"

Monica said, "No, but I have all the information for you."

She rolled her eyes toward the ceiling and said, "Just one moment, I have to go in the back to bring my supervisor in on this one. All the years I've worked here, no one has ever wrecked a car. Were you speeding or something?"

Monica said, "I wasn't the one driving. I'm just listed as the second driver of the car. I really didn't have any intention of driving, but in case I wanted to, I wanted both of us insured."

"Then where is the driver?"

"She's in the hospital. After I get another car, I'll be picking her up."

"Did I hear you say another car? We have a convention in town, there are no more cars."

"Oh Linda, what am I going to do? Christa isn't going to want to ride with you."

"I'm going to the car to call Brandon. I'll let you take his car, leave it at the airport and when he comes in, he can go to the garage and locate it. All I need is for you to call me and let me know where you parked it."

"But Linda, you don't have to go to all that trouble for us."

"Yes I do. Now go on and take care of your business, while I sit in the car and make my call to Brandon."

"Brandon, there is a convention here, so Monica can't get another rental. I made the suggestion that she drive your car to the airport. She will call me and tell me where the car is located in the parking garage."

"This is okay with me. My flight has been delayed so I'll be arriving home about two hours later. I'll call you when I get there. How is Brianna doing?"

"Mom and Dad have really enjoyed their time with her. I can't wait for all three of us to be together again. We have so much talking to do."

"Linda, I love you and will see you soon."

"I love you too, bye for now."

Just as I ended the call, Monica came to the car. She was flushed in the face. You could tell that she was angry.

"Linda, the next time I come here, believe me, I'll be driving my own car. That place has gotten on my last nerves. We even had to call Christa so she could answer some of the questions. I thought when you take out insurance, you were covered and the insurance company will take care of it all. I'm so angry! Please, let's talk about something else."

"I take it that everything's been taken care of?"

"Yes."

"Then, come on and drop me off home and then you can take Brandon's car to pick up Christa."

"Monica, you said you had to speak with Christa. Did you tell her that you would be driving Brandon's car?"

"Yes, she didn't have a problem with it. All she wants to do is get home so she could rest. She said she was still in some pain, and that her head was killing her. By the way, she didn't break her arm, she just has a bad sprain."

"Oh thank God! Did she ask about me?"

"Come on Linda, don't push it. She's still a little angry about the comments you made about her precious Bryan."

"Monica, I still say she needs to do a background check

on him! I said it and I mean it. When this things blows over, I pray I'm wrong and he's one of the nicest men in Orlando, Florida."

Monica said, "Linda, I feel the same way because she really does love him. I pray we're wrong! Now let's get this show on the road. I don't want to make her wait too long. And, thanks for letting us use Brandon's car."

"That's what friends are for. We are still friends aren't we?"

Monica and I hugged and said at the same time. "Yes, till the end of time."

Chapter Twenty

Today is Monday. And it sure does feel good having Brandon home and all that drama behind me. I rolled over and noticed Brandon was gone. I looked at the clock and saw it was 9:00 a.m. I said to myself, I can't believe Brandon didn't wake me before he left for work. I want to call Mom to check on Brianna, but I'd better wait for her to call me just in case Brianna is asleep. Brandon was late getting home because he wanted to go by Mom's and Dad's to spend a little quality time with Brianna.

I gathered my things to shower and to be dressed for the day. Just as I was about to leave the room, the phone started to ring.

"Hello."

"Linda, this is Monica. I know you expected me to call last night but I was so tired when I got home. I have so much to tell you. Are you busy?"

"No. I'm working from home today and Mom still has Brianna, so I'm free to talk."

"I didn't go to work today. I'm still a little sore and really didn't feel like it. When our plane landed, I put Christa in a wheelchair and rolled her to where our luggage was."

"You mean Christa is in that bad of-a-shape? You had to push her around in a wheelchair?"

"Yes, she was complaining that her head felt like it was going to blow off. That is, until we were waiting for our luggage. Bryan came in with an arm full of long stem red roses. He must have had about two dozen."

"You said he had at least two dozen roses! Please don't stop, tell me more."

"Christa almost got out that chair and I know she forgot completely about her painful headache. I just stood there looking at her with this con artist."

"I bet he used her money to purchase those roses."

"I bet you are right. Anyway, he got our luggage and brought it to the curve. I wheeled Christa to where he wanted us to stand while he went to get her car."

"What did she say when he left you two alone?"

"She started talking about how thoughtful he was. She said he didn't have to bring her those roses. By doing this, it showed how much he loved and missed her."

"I bet he couldn't bring the car around fast enough."

"When he got there, Christa acted like she couldn't get out of the wheelchair. He gently helped her. I just got into the back seat and was looking out the window. Thinking that I wish I was home with my husband."

"Did Christa and Bryan stay in Jacksonville or did he drive her back to Orlando?"

"While we were on my way home, Bryan said that since Christa was all banged up, what kind of man would he be if he didn't take her home and take care of her."

"I wanted to say, 'where have you been the entire weekend?

She had tried several times to locate you, but no answer'. She never questioned him."

"Maybe, she was going to ask him those questions when they were alone."

"I hope so, she deserves better. It just hurts me to see her so gullible."

"Me too, but what can we do about it?"

"Nothing! Just pray that he isn't a con artist and has her best interests at heart."

"Monica, I'm just sick to my stomach that things turned out the way they did. I pray in time Christa will forgive me and we can be friends again."

"I think time heals all wounds. Just give her some space and she'll come around. I'll keep you posted as to how things are going with her. Most of all, we have to keep lifting each other up in prayer."

"Monica, you are right. You and Christa mean the world to me and I'm not going to let this ruin our friendship. I'm going to continue to remember you both in prayer and sit back and let God handle this situation."

"Now you're talking. I better go and eat something so I can take a pain pill and lay down. I'll be home all day. If you feel like talking, just call me."

"I'll do that. Again, it was so nice seeing you, and maybe Brandon and I will take a long weekend and come down for a visit."

"What do you mean you and Brandon? You better bring Brianna so I can spoil her. Your mother kept her so we could be together. When you come to Jacksonville, I want to spend more time with that cute little angel."

"Thank you. Now get some much needed rest. And remember, I love you!"

"Linda, I love you too. Now you have a good day. I'll call you in a few days to let you know how things are going."

"Thanks and bye."

"Bye for now."

Okay, now to take my shower and get something in my stomach. I almost made it to the bathroom, when the telephone started ringing.

"Hello."

"Linda, this is Mom. Can you come over and get Brianna?"

"Yes, what's the matter?"

"We just got a call. Grandmother had a rough night and she isn't doing any better. They are waiting for your father. They want to take her to the hospital. I don't want Brianna exposed to whatever she has."

"I don't either. I'm on my way!"

Oh Lord, Grandmother is up in age, I pray she is all right. Lord, please take care of her. I don't know what my Dad would do without her.

I got dressed and was on my way out the door, when I thought I heard my land telephone ringing. I walked over to look at the ID, it was Mother Liz. I shook my head and said to myself, out loud; '*not today Mother Liz! I am by no means in the mood for a conversation with you.*'

While driving to get Brianna my thoughts were on Brandon. I know he isn't a large man, but for some reason he looked as though he was losing weight. I don't want to bother him with my concerns. I guess I'll just have to ask Mom if she noticed it when she saw him last night.

Just as I arrived at Mom's, she walked out to greet me.

I jumped out of the car and said, "Mom, you timed that just right."

"No. I was looking out the window while waiting for you. I have all of Brianna's things stacked up by the door. Please come and get them, then I'll help you to get her in the car."

"Mom, I have a question. When you saw Brandon last night, did you think it looked like he has lost a few pounds?"

"I noticed it, but you know how hard he works. I just thought that food was the last thing on his mind."

"You know doctors make the worst patients. I don't want him to worry, but I'm going to try and find a way to ask him if he's noticed his weight loss."

"Linda, I'm sure it isn't anything serious. If so, he knows how to get a physical and see if there's a problem. Please don't get yourself upset for nothing."

"I guess this sudden death with Marilyn, has caused me to worry about losing Brandon and family members. You know death is so final. I was thinking how just last week I had a conversation with Marilyn, then she was gone."

"Linda, I forgot to tell you Brenda called and said Marilyn's family is making arrangements to have a private memorial service one day this week. She said it's for immediate family members only. Brenda said she got invited because she was a long- time employee."

"I guess due to the way she died, I can see how her family doesn't want people standing around gossiping about her. Thanks for telling me. I was wondering if they would be burying her this week."

"Linda, you go on home and I'll let you know about

Grandmother as soon as I know something. I'll call you from the hospital."

"Oh Mom, I heard from Monica. She and Christa are doing okay. Christa's boyfriend, Bryan, met them at the airport with roses for her."

"Roses! Well, I bet that made her feel good. Maybe he's a good guy after all."

"I sure hope and pray he is. Anyway, thanks for keeping Brianna."

"You don't have to thank me. Your Dad and I enjoyed the time we had with her. I'm so happy we live in the same state, so I can spoil her as much as possible."

Chapter Twenty One

Three days have gone by. Not a cloud in the sky, the sun has been shining all week. My grandmother is back in the nursing home. I thank God for healing her body and allowing her to stay here on earth with us a little longer. I found myself smiling and thinking about what a strong lady she is. I'm happy to have her blood.

Mom called to let me know that she and Dad are leaving in the morning for a long weekend trip. She said he was taking her to New Orleans. She said they will be back late Monday afternoon.

I told her this would be good for them both. Dad needs to get away from the office and Mom needs to be away from the house and spend some quality time with him.

Since Brianna is asleep, I'll call Mother Liz. I know she has probably called Brandon at work by now.

"Good morning Mother Liz."

"Hi Linda, how's my son and granddaughter doing these days?"

"They're both doing great!"

"What made you call me on a Thursday?"

"I just wanted to say hello and to let you know we're

doing good."

"We're going to a medical convention with Olivia's parents. They are taking their private plane and asked us to join them. We don't have to be there until Monday, but we're leaving Saturday so we have a few days to tour the place."

"That sounds like fun. I'll ask Brandon to call you this evening. I know he would like to hear all about it."

"He already knows! I had this conversation with him this morning. You see, I called him and he returned my call immediately."

To get her off my case, I just changed the subject. "Oh! Have you heard from Lynda lately?"

"Yes. She and Carlos are on a seven-day cruise. She called me just before boarding the ship. I got a little upset that she took the baby with them. I told her I could have stayed home to keep him for them. She didn't want to bother me with that. I had to remind her that I am the grandmother and it wouldn't have been any trouble at all."

"I'm sure she knows that, but she probably just wanted to take little Carlos with them. Where did they go?"

"I think she said Mexico. Yes, somewhere in Mexico."

"Mother Liz, I better go and check on Brianna. I just wanted to say hello. Please tell Daddy Alexander that I called and send my love."

"I'll do just that. He's kind of excited about getting away for a few days. At my age, I'm content with my bridge club meeting and just staying home, but not him, he wants to start traveling in and out of the United States."

"I personally don't see anything wrong with that."

"You wouldn't. You don't have to do all the packing and

making sure everything is taken care of. Brandon helps you quite a bit, whereas Mr. Alexander wouldn't lift a finger to help."

Now to end this conversation before she upsets me. "Okay, have a nice trip and I'll kiss Brianna for you."

"You do just that. Thanks for calling. Bye."

"Bye, Mother Liz."

Dear God, no matter how nice I try to be with that lady, at the end of the call, she always has a way of making me feel bad. I guess when things are going well in your life, sometimes a storm comes in to upset your day.

While peeping in to see if Brianna awake, I saw that she was holding up her head and looking around. "Hi Brianna, Mama sees you looking for her. I know you're probably wet and ready to eat. I'll change you and take you in the kitchen while I get you a nice warm bottle."

While feeding Brianna her nice warm bottle, I looked over at the clock to see what time it was. Almost noon! No wonder my stomach is making all kinds of noise. I haven't eaten anything yet today. I had a cup of coffee with Brandon before he left, but he didn't want any breakfast because he had an early surgery. He doesn't like to eat just before surgery.

"Come on Brianna, I'll put you in your carrier while I fix myself a grilled ham and cheese sandwich. I'll take the sandwich and you to my office. After I eat, I can do some work and you can swing until you fall asleep again."

While sitting at my desk clicking away, working, my mind ran across the conversations I had with Mother Liz and Mom. Both are getting away to spend some fun time with their mates. I think I'll see if Brandon is on call in about two weeks. If not, that would be a good time for just the two of us to take a road trip. We could leave on a Friday morning and drive to Hilton Head, South Carolina.

I can see us now, renting a nice condo right on the beach. While Brandon is asleep, I'm not doing any cooking, so I could go out and get us breakfast. When he wakes I could have it all set up for us to eat on the deck. We could feel the warm rays of the sun, and smell the sea, all while watching the waves. In the evenings, we could visit the local restaurants. After dinner, walk the beach and look at the stars.

Wow! I find myself actually sitting here typing and smiling at the same time. I'd better forget the beach and get this work done so I can forward it to Dad.

Startled, I heard the garage door opening. Oh my goodness! I've been working so hard that I have lost track of time. Brianna, who I thought was my time clock, has slept right through while I was working.

"Linda, honey, I'm home!"

"Brandon, I'm in here in my office."

He lean down to kiss me and then he walked over to the carrier and kissed Brianna. She smiled when she opened those big beautiful eyes.

"I came through the kitchen and there isn't a pot on the stove. Are you going to cook something for dinner or are we doing carry out tonight?"

"I've had quite a busy day. I had a conversation with your mother. She said they are leaving with Olivia's parents for a conference in two days."

"Yes, she said Dad was pretty excited about the trip, but she could take it or leave it."

"My parents are going to New Orleans for a few days. Oh, did you know that your sister and Carlos are on a cruise?"

"Yes, Mom told me all about it. She said I should take you away for a week."

"Your Mother said that about me?"

"Yes! I told you the old lady was coming around to loving you as her favorite daughter-in-law."

"What do you know? I thank God for answering my prayers. And by the way, I'm her only daughter-in-law!"

We both had a big laugh about that. "Brandon, do you feel like Chinese tonight?"

"I'm more tired than hungry. If you order it, I'll pick it up."

"No. You take your shower. I'll order it and have it delivered. The delivery boy and I are on first name basis. He'll be here in no time.

"Yes, that's all you ate in your last few months. I thought Brianna was going to be born with slanted eyes."

"Brandon, you go on and get ready. The food will be here in about twenty minutes."

I called and ordered a small amount of food. I really didn't want any left over. I had taken some steaks out and they were marinating for dinner tonight, but I ran out of time to prepare them before he got home. I'll make sure that doesn't happen tomorrow because I'm going to get up early, complete my work, then spend the rest of the afternoon preparing all the food he likes. I'm concerned that he's starting to complain about being tired and he really isn't eating much.

Brandon came to the table dressed in his silk pajamas with his matching robe. He looked as handsome as ever. He just stood there looking at me.

"Why Mr. Brandon, why are you looking at me this way?"

"I'm just standing here feeling awful blessed. I've read the Bible and I know the story of Ruth. I finally feel like Bo'az. I'm sure when he first laid eyes on Ruth, he probably said Wow!"

"Brandon, you need to read your Bible. He didn't say Wow! He said to his servant that was over the reapers, 'Whose damsel is this?'"

"Well, my damsel, shall we dance or shall we eat?"

"What has gotten into you?"

"Can't a man appreciate what God has blessed him with?"

"Yes. Now sit down and bless this food before it turns cold."

Chapter Twenty Two

This is the day that the Lord has made, I will rejoice and be glad in it. Since Brandon is at work, Mom and Dad are on their vacation, and Mother Liz and Daddy Alexander are away, the best thing for me to do is leave the house. Essie wanted to come by and do the housekeeping today, so I won't be in her way.

"Come on, Brianna, let's get our clothes on and hit the mall. We might even take in a movie if one catches my eye."

After we were dressed, fed and ready for the day. I stuffed her bag with everything so I didn't have to go by the grocery store. "Brianna I'm going to sit you right here. I'm going to take your bag to the car."

"Hello Linda. How are you this sunny Saturday morning?"

"Oh! Essie, I didn't even see you. My mind is elsewhere. I'm—I'm doing well by the grace of God."

"I'm sorry I frightened you. I guess I thought you heard me walking."

"No. I was so busy trying to get Brianna's things in the car, so I can hurry back to get her."

"Are you going to your Mother's house?"

"No. She and my Dad are on a mini vacation. I even got a

call from Brandon's mother two days ago and they are leaving sometime today. I guess one of these days Brandon and I will get away."

"You know Linda, if you do want to get away and your parents are not in town, just call me I'll be more than happy to babysit Brianna."

"Thank you, Essie. I'll keep that open invitation in mind. I'd better get her, so we can be on our way. You take care and have a good day."

I strapped Brianna in her car seat, started the car, and popped in my gospel music. We were on our way for a day of fun.

The music was ministering to my soul. While sitting there waiting for the light to turn green. I found myself looking in the mirror, singing alone with the artist. "Brianna, I am in a good mood today and I'm not going to let anyone take my joy!"

We arrived at the mall. I smiled because I landed a parking space near the entrance. This is perfect! I can take my time, get Brianna's stroller out of the trunk, hang her baby bag on it and we'll be ready to shop.

"Come on Brianna, we are going to see what's on sale." Pushing her through the heavy glass doors, I noticed a commotion in the center of the mall. As we got closer, I saw it was a fashion show. I stood there watching the little ones model. It was fun watching them on the cat walk. Some even had their hands on their hips. They were all ages and sizes. "Brianna, just think one of these days you'll be old enough to enter and I'll be sitting by the stage with a big smile on my face just like these parents."

We had almost covered the entire mall. I looked down at my bags and knew it was time to call it a day. I walked, ate, and pushed this stroller and now I was too tired for a movie. By now Essie has completely cleaned the house, so I can get home in plenty of time to prepare dinner for Brandon.

Thinking of Brandon, he hadn't called me once. Hmm, this just isn't like him. I sat on a bench and tried to call him. Looking in my purse I saw everything but my cell phone! That is just not like me to go anywhere without it. Now when was the last time I had it in my hands?

Since I don't have a phone, I have to go home. "Come on Brianna, let's go by the bakery for a dessert. Then home so I can cook dinner."

We arrived home and just as I thought, Essie's car was gone. I pulled in the garage. "Come on, Brianna, I have to take you inside first. I'll come back and get all these bags and the dessert."

After getting her settled in, I brought in all my things. I lay her in her carrier. I went into my office and got her swing and brought it to the family room. I was starting to feel a little tired so I sat down to put my feet up, when I noticed the light on our answering machine flashing.

I pressed the button. "You have 3 messages."

"Message one: "Linda, this is Olivia, I hope you can understand me. I can't seem to reach Brandon. I have an emergency. My parents' plane crashed shortly after take off. Please call me on my cell phone."

Oh my goodness! Did I hear her say plane crashed? Oh my God! I don't want to hear the other messages. I need to call Brandon now! I bet he has been calling me all day.

Where is my cell phone anyway?

I ran to the nursery. I was looking around and there it was—sitting on Brianna's dressing table. Oh my goodness! Brandon's parents were on that plane with them. My fingers were trembling. All I thought about was the death of Marilyn, Christa falling out with me, and now this!

Okay, Linda. Take a deep breath. Now wipe the tears out of your eyes and look at the missed calls. One! And it's from Brandon's parents. I bet it's Mother Liz! She was probably was calling to tell us goodbye. I can't listen to her voice. No, I need to speak to Brandon first.

Walking back to the family room, all I could do was think about how Brandon would feel. Does he even know? Olivia may have only called this number. I better sit down and try calling the hospital. He's probably making his rounds.

I reached for the phone when Brianna started crying. I said to her, "Not now, Brianna. Mommy can't hold you. I need to make a serious call. Sorry, honey."

"Hello. My name is Linda Alexander and I would like to speak with Dr. Brandon Alexander."

The lady on the other end seemed as if she was whispering. I said to her, "Did you hear me? My name is Linda Alexander. I'm the wife of Dr. Brandon Alexander and would like very much to speak with him."

Again, she said something but I couldn't make out the words. I know I've been crying but my ears are not stopped up. I said again, "Ms. Can you hear me?"

She said loud and clear, "Mrs. Alexander. I'm sorry we seemed to have had a bad connection. I've been told that your husband is in surgery right now. I'll have him call you when he gets out."

I sat there thinking if that was me on the operating table wouldn't I want my surgeon to be told that his wife was on the phone and that it was an emergency. I said, "Yes! Yes! Please have him call home right away."

Oh my goodness, here I am with no one to talk with. Mom and Dad aren't here. What do I do? I know, I can always pray. I immediately fell down on my knees and I started calling on the name of the Lord. Even though tears were streaming down my face, and my voice seemed to be getting hoarse, I could clearly hear the words coming out stronger and stronger. I could actually feel my soul crying out to God.

I must have been praying for a while because when I got off my knees, I looked over and Brianna was asleep. Also, I started to feel calm. I knew in my heart that no matter what had happened, God was still in control. Then the telephone rang.

Though my voice was hoarse, I was able to say, "Hello."

"Linda, this is Brandon. What's happening? Linda, are you crying?"

"Yes. You have to come home. I need to speak with you."

"Is it you? Is it Brianna?"

"Brandon, I can't go into it just now. All I can say is please drive carefully and come home now if you can."

"I'm on my way!"

Lord, please take care of him. Please bring him home safely. I just lost my in-laws and I sure don't want to lose my husband.

Chapter Twenty Three

Brandon ran in looking as if he was out of breath. I called out to let him know that we were in the family room.

"Linda, are you all right?"

I stood up and he leaned in my open arms and just held me close.

"Brandon, just hold me. And let's have a word of prayer."

Brandon held me and whispered a prayer. When he stopped I looked him in his eyes and said, "Sit down, first. I have some news. We got a call today from Olivia."

"Olivia?"

"Just one moment—let me finish. Yes, Olivia called to say that her parents' plane crashed on take off."

Brandon stood straight up and raised both hands in the air. He then let them drop to his side and said, "No, No, No! Are you sure? My parents were on that plane. Have you heard from any one else?"

"We had three messages but I only listened to one. Push the button and listen to the other two before calling Olivia.

Message two: "Brandon or Linda, this is Mom. I woke up with one of those terrible migraine headaches. This one was so bad that I was sick to my stomach. I just wanted you both to know that I'm not leaving for the conference right away. If I feel better I'll fly out Sunday. I tried to get your father to go without me, but he insisted on staying home to take care of me. If you need us, please call. Love you, Mom."

"Linda, this means Mom and Dad weren't on the plane. Let's listen to the other message to see who it's from."

Message three: "Brandon, Linda, this is Mom. I don't know if you've heard or not but Olivia's parents are dead! Their plane crashed on take off. Oh my God! We were supposed to be on that flight. I'll try calling your cell phones. When you get this message call me."

Brandon and I sat there looking at each other in silence. Just as I was about to say something, Brianna started crying. Brandon picked her up and held her close to his chest.

Without saying anything, I left to make her a warm bottle, feeling like he needed the time alone.

When I reached the kitchen there was a note on the counter next to the refrigerator. The note was from Essie. It read, "Linda, look in the refrigerator and you'll see a small pan of chicken and rice casserole. I made a pan for my family last night and one for you and Brandon. In the red bowl is a tossed garden salad. Look in the freezer and you'll see the garlic bread. I didn't make any desserts, so you are on your own with that. I know you have been busy and I just wanted to surprise you. Enjoy! Essie."

I said to myself, *Thank you Essie for looking out for us.* I think I'll put the pan in the oven at 350 degrees. I'll make some bottles for Brianna and hopefully after Brandon makes his calls, he will feel like eating a little.

When I walked back to the family room with a nice

warm bottle for Brianna, Brandon was on the phone with someone. I took Brianna from him to change and feed her.

I sat there listening at the conversation. He was talking with his mother. He was choking back the tears. I got up to leave, when he motioned with his hand to stay.

Brandon finally ended the call to his mother. He said, "Linda, Mom is not taking this well at all. She is quite upset over this accident. They were friends forever! She asked when we can go up to be with Olivia. You do know that she's an only child?"

"My heart goes out to her. Brandon, have you tried calling her?"

"Yes, I tried first, but it went right to her voice mail."

"I think your mother is right. You need to go tomorrow and make plans to leave as soon as possible."

"You mean 'we' leave, don't you?"

"I'm thinking she would need someone to go with her to make the arrangements first. Why don't you go to help out with that. Brianna and I can come to the service."

"If that's what you want to do."

"I think that would be best. I know, you probably don't feel like eating, but you do have to keep up your strength. Essie was kind enough to make a chicken and rice casserole. I've put it in the oven to warm for dinner. I'll go and set the table."

"Let me take a shower first. I really don't feel like eating, but I've been so busy that I don't remember the last time I've eaten. Take Brianna and I'll follow you with her swing."

After his shower, Brandon came to the table with a worried look on his face. I tried talking about my day; he just listened. He looked at me and occasionally smiled. I knew that he was only being polite. His mind was really elsewhere. I know that he and Olivia had been friends since childhood, so losing her parents are like losing a part of his family.

Brandon ate most of his food. He looked at me and said, "Please tell Essie the casserole was delicious. I just couldn't eat it all."

"I'll be sure to tell her. Are you going to the family room to watch TV?"

"No. I think I'll try calling Olivia again. If I don't reach her, then I'm going to turn in early."

"Okay, just leave Brianna in here with me. I'll clean up and then take her to my office. I have a little unfinished work that I need to fax to the office in the morning."

After I took care of business and Brianna, I went into our bedroom only to find Brandon tossing and turning. I knew this was going to be a restless night.

"Brandon, I know you aren't asleep. Did you get to talk with Olivia?"

"Yes, she's devastated. I told her that I would be making arrangements to fly there either tomorrow evening or the next day."

"Do you think I should call her and have a word of prayer with her?"

"No. I think we should just keep her lifted up in prayer. She's not herself right now. She just kept saying, why, why, why God took her parents like that."

"What did you say after that?"

"I just kept quiet and let her do the talking. I didn't want her to feel like I have all the answers because I don't. I know she's hurting really badly and I didn't want her to lash out at me because I do still have my parents."

"I think you did the right thing. She has to understand that we came into this world but not to stay. Mrs. Carrie O. used to say, 'This place is not our home. We're just travelers passing through.' Is Olivia home alone?"

"No. Mom, Dad, and some of her church family are with her. She said it is like living in a fog. She can't believe this has happened."

"Brandon, this is why I said you need to get there as quickly as possible. I'm going to make you a cup of sleeper's tea; it might help to calm you down."

"Linda, I don't need you to go to all that trouble I'll be all right."

"Brandon, it's no trouble at all. After you drink the tea, we'll have prayer together and just know that God is still in control and He will take care of everything."

Chapter Twenty Four

Brandon was in the kitchen with his head hung low. He was drinking a cup of coffee. I walked in and he never looked up.

"Good morning Brandon."

He slowly raised his head and said, "Good morning Linda. Did I wake you?"

"No. I tossed and turned most of the night just like you did. My mind was on Olivia. May I fix you something light to eat?"

"No. I had a glass of orange juice and this black coffee is all I want."

"Do you want me to call the airline and make reservations for you?"

"No. I'm going in early to do that. Are you going to church this morning?"

"Yes. With all of this that has happened, I need to hear the Word."

"Linda, I better go. After I see my patients, I'm coming straight home to start packing. I know I should be able to get a flight out early this evening. I'll make sure it would be after you get out of church."

"Okay. Give me a kiss and I'll see you later."

After I fed and dressed Brianna I spent most of the morning looking on the internet for a direct flight. Either Brandon had to stay in the airport for a couple of hours, or he would have two layovers. I couldn't find a nonstop flight.

"Brianna I'd better get off this computer and get ready for church. Come on Brianna, it smells like you need to be changed again."

As I was leaving the office, the phone rang. I said to myself, "How am I going to get this? I have you, Brianna in one hand and your dirty diaper in the other." By the time I put her down, the phone had stopped ringing.

I went to look at the Caller ID, it was Monica. I'd better not get caught up talking to her. I need to get myself ready for church. I'll call her after Brandon leaves tonight.

Brianna and I got to church a little late. The choir had already marched in and the church clerk was giving weekly announcements. One of the friendly ushers asked if I wanted to sit up front, but I told her no. I asked that she please seat us three rows from the back.

I sat down and took Brianna out of her carrier. I was about to place her on my lap when a little old lady sitting next to me asked if she could hold her. I smiled and passed Brianna right to her.

The choir sang two spirit-filled selections. The spirit was high and I was happy to be in the midst. When it was time for prayer, I asked the lady if she wanted me to let her pass, so she could go to the altar for prayer. I was hoping she didn't want to go so I could leave Brianna with her, while I went to pray for Olivia.

The little old lady said, "Do I mind? I don't even know you. I just wanted to hold this pretty little girl. She looks just like my daughter did when she was a little baby. Look next to me, this here is my daughter. "

She turned and looked at the lady sitting next to her. She said, "Wanda, introduce yourself to this here nice lady."

The lady said, "Please excuse my mother. I know its prayer time and she's hard of hearing and is in the first stage of dementia. If you want to go up for prayer, I'll stay here and watch her with your little girl."

I leaned forward to introduce myself. I said, "My name is Linda Alexander and I would like very much to go up for prayer. Thank you for keeping my baby. By the way, her name is Brianna."

I made my way to the altar for prayer. As the assistant preacher prayed, I asked God to bless my entire family. I also asked if He would please be with Olivia during this trying time in her life.

I walked back to my seat. The little old lady was talking to Brianna, but this time she was getting a little louder. Her daughter patted her on the knee to let her know that she was getting a little too loud. She also reminded her they were in church and it was time for the minister to deliver his speech.

I reached for Brianna and thanked her for watching her. She was so happy to have been helpful because she said not one but twice, the next time I come to church to be sure and sit with her so she could take care of Brianna.

I gave Brianna a bottle and before long she was fast asleep. I was able to listen to the sermon and enjoyed it very much.

After the service I gathered Brianna and was ready to get

home to help Brandon pack. The old lady said for me to sit with her next Sunday. I told her I'd make sure and look for her the next time I came to church.

Her daughter said, "I couldn't help but to notice that during the sermon you were crying a lot. I don't mean to get in your business, but I want to say that anyone who is as kind to my mother as you are, has a good heart. I have a solution—take your problems to God and I promise you He'll take care of them. It isn't easy trying to take care of my mother in this condition, but I can truly say that God has been an anchor for me."

"Thank you Wanda. I'll remember what you have shared with me today. I also want you to know that I meant what I said to your mother. The next time I come to church I'll be looking to sit with her."

"She might not remember you, but I don't think she'll forget this beautiful little girl."

"Thank you, again, it was nice meeting you."

Brianna and I hurried home to see Brandon before he left for the airport. When I got inside, he was sitting in the family room with his leg crossed.

"Brandon, are you packed and ready to go?"

"Yes, you timed it just right. I have just enough time to kiss you and hold Brianna. My plane leaves in three hours. I'll call you when I get to my parent's house."

"Okay. Have you eaten?"

"Yes, I had a BBQ sandwich and bought you a dinner. It's on the stove."

"Thanks. I'll walk you to the car."

Brianna and I stood there watching him as he put his

suitcase in the trunk. He was moving as if he was really tired. I guess he really has a lot on his mind. He walked over and hugged me and kissed both of us goodbye.

We watched and waved until we couldn't see him. I felt my eyes filling up with tears. "Come on, Brianna, let's get out of these church clothes and get comfortable. I have some good BBQ waiting for me."

After dinner I wanted so much to call my mother to let her know about Olivia's parents and what almost happened to Brandon's parents, but I didn't. No need to spoil their vacation. Instead, I went to bedroom to look for a good book.

A thought came to me. *I owe Monica a call and since Brianna is in her swing, this is a good time to make that call.*

The phone rang and rang. Finally, she picked up.

"Hello. Monica, this is Linda."

"Hi, Linda, things are going great! I knew you were calling me because earlier you probably saw my number on your Caller ID. Let me explain. It really wasn't me calling. It was Christa."

"Christa? Is she there with you in Jacksonville?"

"No. She didn't want you to flip out, so she asked me to call you and then flash her in so we all were on three-way. Since you weren't home she told me the entire story."

"Story! I think the first thing out of her mouth should be an apology. She really didn't act like herself when she was here."

"Yes, you're right. I think she is going to do that too. But first, you'll have to call her so she can tell you everything."

"You keep saying the entire story, everything. Does this have anything to do with Bryan?"

"Everything! now, call her."

"I'll call her, but I wanted to tell you that Olivia's parents were killed in a plane crash and Brandon's parents were supposed to be on the plane with them."

"What? This is the girl Mother Liz is so crazy about. The one she wanted Brandon to marry. Oh, my heart goes out to Olivia. I'm so sorry she lost her parents like this."

"Yes, she's the one, but she and Brandon have a sister and brother relationship. Anyway, he flew out to be with her and his parents. I'll be joining him later when they make the funeral arrangements. I'll keep you posted, but right now I have to make this call to Christa. You have piqued my interest with what's going on between Christa and Bryan. I'll talk with you later. Thanks and love you!"

"Love you too. Bye."

Chapter Twenty Five

I thought before I made this call, I should have a little talk with God. "Lord, I don't want Christa and me to be enemies. I want us to be friends like we used to be. When I call, I pray she's back to her old self. Lord, if I've done anything to cause her to act differently, please forgive me. Thank you!"

My fingers were actually shaking, probably because she really wasn't herself the last time we were together. I dialed the number and waited for her to answer.

Christa finally answered and said, "Hello. Linda, how are you?"

"I guess you saw my number on your Caller ID."

"Yes, I did. First of all, Linda, I have to ask you to please forgive me for the way I conducted myself while I was in your home. When I look back at how I acted, I just allowed the devil to use me for his glory. I really did act up and I'm sorry."

"Christa, I know you weren't yourself. You really don't have to apologize. I'm the one who should apologize for giving you my opinion of Bryan. I just want the best for you. I mean, he just may be the best person for you."

"Linda, please let me talk. When I came to Georgia, I was happy to have Bryan in my life. I thought the world of him. I let him use my car anytime he asked. I would go as far as making sure it was full of gas. When I was there and you talked about doing a background check on him, I thought that was terrible. When I came home from visiting you, he had the nerve to be waiting at the airport with roses. I probably was the one to buy them. Yes, he had access to my debit card, but I was smart enough to give him the one that only had a limited balance—which he wiped out."

"You mean he used your car and took your money?"

"Let me finish. I'm so ashamed I can't believe I'm confessing all of this to you. When we took Monica home and were driving back to Orlando, he kept saying how he was going to take care of me. He said he has been looking for a steady job. I was in so much pain that I really wasn't listening to all of his empty promises. To make a long story short, I got on the internet and paid for some valuable information. Bryan is a crook and I got him out of my life forever. I even went downtown and took out a restraining order against him. I'm so ashamed of how I treated you. Can you ever forgive me?"

"Christa, we are friends forever. I forgive you. I'm just happy that God opened your eyes and that things were not worse. He could have led you down the wrong path- like marriage."

"Yes. He kept bringing up the subject."

"Christa, like I said, you weren't yourself and now you're back. All you have to do is stay prayerful and let God find you a mate. The internet is no place for a good Christian lady like you! "

"Yes. I promised myself that I wasn't going to look up a

man on the computer, again. I am going to wait for God to bless me with one. That way, I'll be equally yoked."

"You can say that again. Christa, you remember Olivia don't you?"

"Yes, she's the lady your mother-in-law wanted Brandon to marry."

"Well, her parents and Brandon's parents were supposed to fly to a conference together in their private plane."

"You didn't tell me Mother Liz had a private plane."

"She doesn't! It was Olivia's parents' plane. Anyway, they were going to this conference and the plane crashed on take off."

"Did anyone get killed?"

"Yes, that's what I'm trying to tell you. Olivia's parents were the only ones on the plane. Mother Liz became ill so they stayed home. Brandon left to be with her and his family."

"You two must have a strong marriage. I wouldn't let my husband be in the company of his old girlfriend without me."

"Christa, are you trying to get back at me?"

"Linda, all I'm saying is you trust him completely. You are willing to let him be with a grieving old girlfriend."

"Christa, first of all, Olivia and Brandon have a sister-brother relationship. They went to the same schools. The loss of her parents is just like Brandon losing a family member. I trust Brandon completely. I have faith that he will always conduct himself like a married man, whether I'm with him or not!"

"Are you raising your voice at me? Did I hit a nerve?"

"No you didn't. I just want to be perfectly clear to you that I have nothing to worry about."

"Linda, I'm just playing with you, girl. Anyway, I'm sorry for her loss and I'd better get off the phone. It sure was good talking with you. Again, please accept my apology because you know that it really wasn't you that I was upset with- it was Bryan."

"I know, and it's so good having you back in my life. I'll talk with you when I get back from being with Brandon's parents. I'll probably need your shoulder to cry on, after being with Mother Liz."

"Who knows, since she came so close to death, she just might become a changed lady. I mean a lady who respects other people's feelings."

"Christa, I hope you are right about her. I'd better get going. Brianna is in her swing asleep and I need to put her in her crib. Again, it was so nice talking with you. We will get together real soon."

"You said real soon. Well, sooner than you think. I was saving the best for last. I'm moving back to Jacksonville."

"Jacksonville? Now you have really made me happy."

"When I told my parents, they were so happy they offered to let me live with them. I told them just for a little while because I need to have my own space."

"I know Monica is one happy lady to have you back with her."

"Yes, she keeps trying to get me to give her a definite date, but first I have to get my business in order. I do know that it will be a couple of months."

"Okay. I'll say bye for now! Love you."

"Linda, I love you too."

I know Christa's parents can sleep easier knowing that

she's on her way back home and out of harm's way with Bryan.

After hanging up the phone, I wondered how much fun Mom and Dad were having. I would like to hear from them, but I won't call to let them know about Olivia's parents, and what almost happened to Brandon's parents. I know that would spoil their trip.

I think I'll go in my office to answer some of my emails. I can get a lot done while Brianna is asleep. First, I'd better take one last look to see how she's doing before heading to the office. When I peeked in, she was moving around. I stood there waiting for her to either wake up or go back to sleep.

Brianna reached for her pacifier and put it in her mouth. She finally went back to sleep, so I tiptoed to the office. I logged on and was about to do some work, when I decided to see if I had any personal emails. I got a notice that Monica was online. I knew this was going to be a long conversation. We started chatting about both of our conversations with Christa.

I looked at the clock and noticed that Monica and I had been online for more than two hours. I told her that I needed to get off and make a call to Brandon. By now, his plane had landed. He must have forgotten to call me.

I called Brandon and was surprised that he didn't answer. I tried calling his cell phone again, this time I let it ring until it went to voice mail.

"Brandon, this is Linda. I've been waiting to hear from you. Please let me know that you are arrived safely and how your parents and Olivia doing."

I picked up Brianna because she was crying and I knew by now she was hungry. After changing her, we went to the kitchen to make a nice warm bottle.

After the bottle was ready, I took Brianna to the family room and turned on the TV to try to find something interesting. I needed something to keep me up until I heard from Brandon.

It was close to midnight and not a word from Brandon. I didn't think I should try and call him this late. "Come on, Brianna, let's get ready for bed. Who knows, so much probably has happened since your Daddy arrived that he forgot to call home to check on us."

Chapter Twenty Six

While lying here trying to get a little more sleep, I couldn't help but notice how bright the sun was shining through the blinds. I pulled the covers over my eyes, but it didn't seem to help. I looked towards the nightstand to see what time it was. It was a little after seven. I didn't want to do much moving around because Brianna was right next to me.

I eased out of bed and put a pillow on each side of her, so I could go to the bathroom to freshen up. When I came out, she was still sleeping. I grabbed the cordless phone and went back to the bathroom to call Brandon.

Brandon answered on the second ring. He was whispering in the phone. He said, "Linda, please don't be angry with me. I arrived here and my mother was a wreck. I spent most of the time trying to console her. Olivia was given a sedative, so she doesn't even know that I'm in town."

"Brandon, I waited and waited for you to call me, but now I understand. How is she now that you are there?"

"She's a little better. I haven't seen her this morning. It's still pretty early. I was in the kitchen trying to make a pot of coffee, so when everyone gets up they can have a cup. I just don't know where things are in this house."

"You mean you don't remember where your parents keep

things? And why are you whispering?"

"No, what I'm trying to say is we all stayed with Olivia at her parent's house."

"Olivia?"

"Yes, my parents didn't want to leave her alone. You can understand their concerns, can't you?"

"Yes. What are your plans for today?"

"I think we are all going with Olivia to make funeral arrangements. Mother said Olivia wants to get this behind her. She would like to have a memorial service for them this Wednesday."

"Did you say Wednesday? Brandon, that's in two days!"

"This is just the information I got from my mother. I haven't seen Olivia yet. If she does have it in two days, you'll just have to make reservations to fly out tomorrow. I'll call you later after the final arrangements are made."

"Oh Brandon, I wish I was there with you. You sound so sad."

"Linda, I wish you were here with me. How's Brianna?"

"She's like me, we're both missing you."

"I know. Just go online and see if you're able to find a direct flight. My flight had two layovers. That will be hard for you, trying to handle Brianna. I wish your parents were home so they could keep her."

"I wish they were home too. I'll get online now, while she's still asleep. You go on and I'll wait to hear from you. Love you and keep your chin up. You have got to be strong for your mother and Olivia."

"I know. You'll be hearing from me today. Linda, I love you. Kiss the baby for me and tell her that I love her."

"I will. Bye."

"Bye."

The sound of his voice made me feel sad and lonely. I know Brandon is a mama's boy and to hear him like that made me wish I was there with him. If Brianna is still sleeping, then I'll go online to see what flights are available.

While in the office on the computer looking for flights I thought I heard Brianna crying. I stopped clicking the keys to listen. Yes, she was crying and was now starting to get pretty loud. I immediately logged off so I could tend to her needs.

After taking care of her and eating a bowl of cereal, we both went back to the computer to check more airlines to see if they had any available flights.

In between, I spent most of the day checking different airlines for a seat on a plane leaving tomorrow. I even tried to call Essie. Each time the calls would go in her voice mail. I left a message for her to call me immediately.

After searching, I was not able to find a direct flight. There were only two seats left with quite a long layover between flights. I knew these wouldn't work for me if I had to take Brianna with me, but I don't want to book it without talking to Essie first, because they are non-refundable tickets.

I was giving Brianna a bottle when Essie finally called. I reached over to hit the speaker button.

"Hello Essie."

"Hi. Linda. I see that you have been calling me. I'm so sorry I am just now getting back with you. We are out of town at an amusement park and won't be leaving until Wednesday."

"Did I hear you say Wednesday?"

"Yes, is something wrong?"

"Yes, Brandon is also out of town. He's in Massachusetts with his parents to attend a funeral Wednesday and wanted me to join him. I tried calling the airlines but the flights are too long for me to sit in the airport with Brianna."

"Oh, I wish I was there to keep her for you."

"I do too."

"Please forgive me for just now returning your calls. My cell phone was in my purse and we have been riding almost all the rides and I guess I didn't hear it. What made me call you now is because I took my phone out to call the children to meet me for something to eat. They are smarter than me, they said they would put their phones on vibrate so they could feel it when it rang."

"That's okay Essie, you and your family enjoy yourselves. I'll think of something. Thanks for calling me back and I pray you have a safe trip back home."

"Okay. Bye."

I hung the phone up feeling awfully bad. Part of me wanted to risk taking Brianna and part of me didn't feel like being troubled with the stroller and staying at the airport all those hours. I called Brandon to see if the funeral would be on Wednesday.

"Hello Brandon. Has Olivia made the arrangements?"

"Yes. I was going to call you after we got back home."

"Is this a good time to talk?"

"Yes. Dad and I are just sitting here while Mom and Olivia are still inside talking with the undertaker. The memorial service will be held at their church on Wednesday.

Were you able to get a flight?"

"There were only two seats left on one airline. The only problem is it had a three hour layover and that is too much time for me to be staying in an airport with Brianna."

"Can you get Essie to keep her?"

"I tried that, but she and her family are out-of-town."

"Brandon. I think I should just get the address of the church and send some flowers from us and stay home. You can tell me all about it when you return."

"Oh. Linda! I just wish you were here with me."

"I know, but it is not workable. I don't mind staying and like I said, you can bring home a program and tell me all about it when you come home. Just tell Olivia that I tried to be there, but I just couldn't make it."

"I know she'll understand. I'll also tell my mother that you tried very hard to be here with us."

"You go on and call me this evening after you get settled before going to bed. Oh, are you still staying at Olivia's?"

"Yes. We all are."

"Okay. I'll talk with you later. I love you!"

"I love you too. Bye for now."

Chapter Twenty Seven

Brandon really does miss me. He has been calling a lot to see how we're doing. He calls in the afternoon and before going to bed. I guess he doesn't want me to feel left out because he's there with Olivia.

It's almost two o'clock and by now I should have heard from him. I guess he hasn't called because they are probably having dinner after the memorial service. I'll take Brianna's swing and we can sit in the backyard while I do a little reading.

Just as I got Brianna all settled and I sat down to read, I heard "Hello. Linda, it's Mom and Dad, are you back here?"

"Mom, Brianna and I are just sitting here enjoying this beautiful day. Give me a hug. You both look so good and rested."

"Linda, we had so much fun! Your father really did enjoy himself. He even took me on a tour to see the cemetery in New Orleans."

"Dad, you couldn't think of a better place to take her? What about the French Quarter? I've seen that place on movies and it's pretty wild."

"We saw it all. I just wanted her to see how they buried their bodies on top of the soil because of the water level."

"Mom, while you're holding Brianna I'll go in and get you both some nice cold ice tea."

"Your father would like the tea. He loves how sweet you make it. I'll just take a bottle of water.

"Linda, do you have anything to go with that tea?"

"Like what? Dad, are you hungry?"

"Yes, I don't like to eat a heavy meal while I'm driving. I sure would like to have one of those turkey and ham sandwiches. You know the ones you make with that marble bread. This time you don't have to toast my bread."

"One turkey and ham sandwich coming right up! Mom would you like something to eat?"

"No. Water is good for me. I have been snacking all the way here. I just want to hold Brianna and enjoy her."

"Vivian, why don't you pass her to me, when Linda brings my sandwich, you can hold her while I eat."

"Okay you two. She's plenty for both of you. Speaking of plenty, Dad, I will be meeting you in the office Monday morning. I have so much to share with you."

"Linda, do you want me to keep Brianna at your house or will you be bringing her to our house?"

"Why don't I bring her to your house and we'll see how that works."

"Okay with me."

"Hmmm, Linda, my stomach is rumbling, the sandwich please."

I rushed to the kitchen to prepare the sandwich for Dad. I even put a pickle and some chips on his plate. I got a bottle of ice cold water for Mom and a tall glass of ice tea for Dad. When I walked out with the tray of goodies, he was still holding and playing with Brianna.

Dad looked up and immediately he gave Brianna to Mom. He then took some of the hand sanitizer that was sitting on the table and rubbed both hands together. He bowed his head for a word of prayer.

He said, "Now that's a sandwich. Linda, you sure do know how to make your old man feel special. Hey, what time will Brandon be home?"

"Oh, I wanted you to first enjoy our company before I sprung the bad news on you."

Dad put his sandwich back on the plate and Mom turned around to see what I was talking about. She said, "Linda, what bad news?"

"Olivia's parents and Brandon's parents were going to a medical conference. Olivia's parents were taking their private plane. Well, Mother Liz became ill and they cancelled the trip. Olivia's parents left, but their plane crashed on take off."

"Linda, what are you saying? Are you saying Olivia's parents are dead?"

"Yes. Today was their memorial service. Brandon is there with her and his parents. He wanted me to be with him, but I couldn't find a direct flight."

"Why didn't you call us? We would have come home right away."

"I know Dad, but I would have had to leave yesterday and no way could you have been here that quick."

"I know Brandon's parents are taking this hard because they were good friends."

"Yes. Brandon said his mother is really taking it hard. I'm just happy that he is there to support her."

"When will he be coming home?"

"Mom, I don't know. He promised to call me tonight to let me know all about the service and when to expect him."

"Linda, if anything like this happens again—I mean anything, you call us. I could have flown your mother home and then took my time and drove home. You really needed to be with Brandon."

"Yes, Sir!"

Mom said, "You know this is sad. Life is so precious. I'm sad that she has lost both of her parents at the same time."

"My heart goes out to her. The only good thing is that she had her parents in her life a long time. God blessed her that she didn't lose them while she was a child."

Dad said, "Another good thing is that she wasn't in the plane with them. She's a medical doctor and the world needs good young doctors."

Mom said, "We will just have to keep her lifted up in prayer that God will be her strength. Linda, you'll have to keep in touch with her. She could use a friend."

"You're right Mom. When Brandon comes home we could invite her to our home to spend a few days. She probably really needs to get away from there."

Mom said, "You two keep on talking. I'm going to take Brianna inside to change her diaper. I think she would like a nice warm bottle of milk."

"Mom, she just had a bottle before we came out here. Maybe you could see if she will take a little water."

"Come on Brianna, I'm home and I know what you like."

Dad and I just looked at each other and started laughing. He said, "She's going to have that baby fat in no time. Now tell me what you have to show me Monday. Do you want to go to your office so I can see the paperwork?"

"No, you're still on vacation. It can wait until Monday."

"Okay. Then can I trouble you for another glass of tea?"

"Why don't I bring the pitcher out? You can then have as much as you want."

"Before you do that, do you have anything sweet? Like a piece of pie or cake?"

"I have some ice cream and chocolate chip cookies."

"I think that would do it."

Mom came back with Brianna and a bottle of water. She said, "What would do it?"

"Dad wanted something sweet. I have some ice cream and cookies."

"The tea is sweet enough and could be considered as a dessert."

Dad said, "You go on Vivian. Just because you're full, you don't want me to be."

"Alphonso, you shouldn't want anymore ice cream. Remember all the flavors you tried in New Orleans?"

Dad said, "Vivian, you don't have to tell her everything I did."

Mom said, "He took me to so many places, and restaurants. I can truly say we had a good time."

"Yes, we did! I'll probably hit the gym after work Monday. Not now! Besides Linda said I'm still on vacation."

Mom and Dad stayed another hour. They enjoyed their visit with Brianna and I enjoyed hearing about their trip.

Brandon finally called. He started out apologizing for not calling right after the service. I had to tell him it was okay and that I understood completely. He read the program to me. He talked about the service and how Olivia was able to express herself by thanking the people for coming. He said it was crowded. He went on and on about how much people cared about both of her parents.

He then got a little sad when he talked about how Mother Liz was handling it. I told him he should stay there a few days longer to be with her. His voice became cheerful. He promised to take a flight home Friday afternoon.

I told him I would take Brianna to Mom and Dad's house, so we could spend some time alone. He was happy about that. He said, though, that he would like to go by their house before coming home. He wanted to spend a little time with Brianna first.

He ended the call by saying how much he loved and missed us.

The next day was a busy day. Mom and I went to visit Grandmother. She was happy about all the attention she got. She especially enjoyed Brianna. After our visit we went to the mall to buy a few outfits for Brianna. Then Mom wanted to go grocery shopping, which was okay with me because I had a few things to buy since Brandon would be home tomorrow. I wanted to surprise him with a nice dinner.

Chapter Twenty Eight

Today is Friday! I'm so happy! In a few hours Brandon will be home. I've already taken Brianna to Mom's for the night. I've marinated the beef for the kebabs. I got the garlicky roasted asparagus, and corn on-the-cob ready. I've peeled the fruit for the fruit salad and need to set the table.

After setting the table on the patio, I stood there to take one last look. Everything was simply beautiful. Look out Martha Stewart, Linda Alexander is in town! I know when Brandon comes home and sees how the table is set and how the food smells, he's going to be one happy man.

I hurried to take a shower so I would be dressed and looking nice when he walked in. After getting dressed and applying my makeup, I took one last look in the mirror and said to myself, "I am ready to meet my man."

I was standing in front of the grill, turning over the beef kebabs, when I felt a familiar pair of hands around my waist. Smiling, I turned and Brandon was all smiles. So was I.

He said, "Hello, beautiful." And he kissed me.

I thought I was going to melt in his arms. It felt like he had been gone for ages. It was so good having him home!

He said, "Everything looks and smell good. How much

time do I have before dinner is ready?"

"Dinner is ready now. All I have to do is bring everything out here."

"Can you wait for two things? I'll like to take my luggage in and grab a quick shower. I want to put on a pair of shorts and get comfortable."

"Okay, that will give me time to bring everything out and make our plates. I'll see you in a few minutes."

Brandon gave me one more kiss, then he picked up his luggage and left.

I was feeling pretty good now. I went inside to get the rolls and the strawberry cake. I wanted so much for this to be an evening he would remember forever.

We spent most of the evening outside talking and laughing. It was like old times before Brianna was born. What made it even more special was the full moon that was shining so bright. As I lay in his arms and listened to the poetry he was reciting, it made me feel how blessed I was and how thankful I was to God for the love that Brandon and I share.

The next morning, the house was quiet and peaceful. I looked over at Brandon, he was still sleeping. I wanted to make him a nice breakfast and serve him in bed. I slowly got out, and softly walked to the bathroom to freshen up. When I came back, he was still lying on his stomach. I tiptoed to the kitchen to turn on the oven. I wanted to have the ham with spinach quiche, hash brown potatoes, and some of the leftover fruit salad.

I was just cooking and singing to myself, when I thought I heard Brandon call out to me. I stopped to listen, but didn't hear anything. I continued to sing softly while making his plate. I wanted the tray to look good so I decorated it with a red rose in a glass vase.

I was ready to pour his coffee, when I looked at the tray and noticed he didn't have any orange juice. After putting the small glass of orange juice on the tray, I was now ready to serve him in bed. A breakfast fit for a king. My king!

I walked back to the bedroom holding the tray when I looked he wasn't in bed.

I called out to him "Brandon, where are you?"

I walked over to his side of the bed and saw he was on the floor. I set the tray down on the bed and said, "Brandon! Brandon! Wake up!"

He didn't move. I started to lightly tap him in his face. I kept yelling his name, "Brandon! Brandon! Can you hear me?"

He was finally able to make some groaning noise. I reached for a pillow off the bed to lay his head on it. I ran to the nightstand to get the phone. I dialed 911.

The operator said, "911 what's your emergency?"

I said, "My name is Linda Alexander and when I came back into our bedroom I found my husband on the floor."

She said, "Is he conscious?"

I said, "He is now." She kept asking me question after question and I found myself getting a little impatient. I gave her our address and asked her to please send an ambulance immediately.

I kept trying to talk to him, but it seemed as if he was going in and out of consciousness. Finally, I heard the sound of the ambulance arriving. I didn't want to leave Brandon, but

I had to open the door for the paramedics.

They rushed to the bedroom and started working on him, so I left to lock the back door. I told the driver that I would be following them to the hospital. I grabbed my purse and ran behind them.

When we arrived, I had to go around the parking lot twice to park the car. Finally, someone came out and I was able to take their spot. I rushed into the emergency room and ran to the admitting desk. I told the clerk who I was and asked if I could go back to where my husband was. She said no. I needed to fill out the paperwork and stay there until the doctors sent for me.

I signed the admitting papers and answered as many questions as I could. I passed them to her and said, "Can I go back there with my husband now?"

She said, "No. I'm still waiting to hear from the doctors. Is there anyone you can call to be with you?"

I said, "Yes! I'll call my parents. Thanks."

I took out my cell phone to call my mother, when it started to ring.

"Hello. Linda, this is Mother Liz. I called your house but no one answered. I even called Brandon's cell phone and still no answer."

Just as I was about to speak, the words got caught in my throat. I swallowed to choke back the tears and said, "Mother Liz, I'm in the emergency room with Brandon."

She yelled, "Emergency room! What's the matter with Brandon?"

"I don't know! I was making his breakfast and when I came back to the room, he was on the floor unconscious."

"Unconscious! When were you going to call us? What are the doctors saying?"

"I haven't been here but a few minutes. I'm still waiting to hear from the doctors. The reason I didn't call is because I really don't know anything yet."

That time I could hear Daddy Alexander in the background. He came on the phone. "Linda, I'm going to call the airlines and we'll be there as soon as possible. I don't want you to feel like you have to go through this all by yourself."

"Daddy Alexander, why don't you wait until I hear from the doctors? Brandon just might be overworked. If this is something minor, then you would have come here for nothing. I'll call you as soon as I hear something."

"You promise?"

"Yes sir!"

"Okay, then I'll be right here by the phone waiting. By the way, Lynda and Carlos are back from their trip."

"Okay, I'll call you later. Bye."

The admitting nurse called me to the desk. She said, "The doctor said he would like to meet with you in the conference room." She pointed to the first small room down the hall on the left.

Now I thought, why the conference room? Why don't they let me see Brandon? Dear God, please take care of Brandon. Please don't take him from me.

While walking to the room I felt as if my knees were going to buckle after making it to the chair. I put my head down for a word of prayer. I was praying to myself, when I heard the doctor clear his throat.

He said, "I'm Dr. McKinney."

I shook his hand and introduced myself saying, "My name is Linda, Linda Alexander and I'm so scared. Please tell me that Brandon is all right."

"He said, "I wish I could. We are still waiting on the blood work. Do you know if your husband's family has a history of renal failure?"

I said, "Renal failure? Do you mean Brandon is having problems with his kidney?"

"Yes. His blood pressure was elevated and his urinalysis showed positive for protein and blood. The microscopic findings showed casts, which means their presence indicates inflammation of the kidneys."

Oh my goodness! I don't know his history. I'll call his parents. But first, can I see him?"

"Yes, but please don't stay long. I would like for you to talk to his parents right away and if possible, let me know something today."

"I'll call them right now."

I called Brandon's parents, and Daddy Alexander answered saying, "Hello."

"Daddy Alexander, this is Linda. I'm here with the doctor. He asked if you or your wife had a history of renal failure."

"No. Is that what he thinks is wrong with Brandon?"

"They're waiting on the blood test results. He said that Brandon's blood pressure was elevated and he has protein and blood in his urine, so he just wanted to know the history."

"Linda, I think Liz and I are on the next plane there. We'll call you after we make the reservations."

"All right, you can call me on my cell phone."

"Well doctor, where we go from here?"

"I'll let you see Brandon. Then we'll have to wait for the blood test results. In the meantime, I'm on call today. You have nothing to worry about. Brandon is in good hands. God will take care of him."

"Thank you. It's good to know that he is being care for by a Christian doctor."

He said, "Thank you. I'll show you to his room."

When I walked in Brandon was just lying there with his eyes closed. I walked over to the side of his bed. I looked down at him and said, "Hi."

He opened his eyes and said, "Hello, Beautiful."

I smiled. I then leaned down to kiss him on his forehead. I said, "I called your parents and they are making reservations to come here."

"Oh. Linda. I'm not in that bad a shape. I think I'm just a little tired."

Dr. McKinney came back in the room and said, "Young man, I have one of your test results and it show that your creatinine is 1.9. I know you're a doctor so you know this means your kidneys are almost working around 50%."

Brandon took a deep breath and just rolled his eyes to the ceiling. He must have looked up for about a minute or two before he answered. He said, "What are you going to do?"

Dr. McKinney said, "I think the first thing is to admit you. In the morning we'll schedule you for a biopsy. After the biopsy, we'll keep you in here for a few days. Then we will probably try you on a prednisone therapy and a blood pressure pill. Hopefully, this may reverse your condition."

I was looking at Brandon and he was just looking as though he was trying to take all of this in. I thought I should be the one to ask the question. I said, "Dr. McKinney, did you say his kidney is working about 50%?"

"Yes."

"Can a person live with a kidney working at that capacity?"

"Yes, but they would not feel normal and would be very tired."

Brandon cleared his throat and said, "If the prednisone therapy doesn't control my creatinine from elevating, what's next?"

Dr. McKinney said, "Let's take this condition one step at a time."

Brandon said, "I'm not worried, because I know who takes care of me. I'm in God's hands. I just don't want to worry my wife.

Dr. McKinney said, "If the prednisone therapy doesn't work, then you might be looking at either dialysis or getting a kidney transplant. Like I said, please don't worry. Let's wait on the biopsy to see what we're facing. I know this is a lot to absorb, so I'm leaving so you and your wife can talk. I'll check on you later, before you're admitted to a room.

I said, "Thank you, Dr. McKinney."

Brandon thanked him too. He then looked up at me with tears welling up in his eyes and said, "Linda, I'm so sorry for this!"

Chapter Twenty Nine

I called my parents to let them know about Brandon. Mom wanted to leave Brianna with Dad and come to the hospital to be with me. I told her that Brandon's parents called and they're here at the airport waiting to rent a car. One good thing is that the hospital is near our house, so after they visit with Brandon, they can go to our home and get some rest.

I called Brandon's sister, Lynda, to let her know his condition. She wanted to fly out in the morning to be by his side. I told her no. Her parents are here. She then asked the question that I was trying to avoid. She said, "Linda, if Brandon's kidneys are destroyed, wouldn't he need a transplant?"

I said, "Yes. I've been sitting here thinking about that. I've also decided to have my blood drawn to see if I'm a match."

I could hear her starting to cry. I said, "Lynda, don't cry. God has Brandon in His hands. He has never left us. He promised to be with us and I know He will."

Lynda blew her nose and said, "I'm sorry for blowing my nose while talking with you, but I just can't hold back the tears. My little brother is lying there not knowing what's facing him! He has to be scared."

"Brandon is stronger than you think. Yes, he's shed a few tears, but his faith in God is what's going to carry him through this storm."

"And you! What a blessing to have such a caring, Christian wife by his side. When you find something out, please call me immediately. Carlos and I really would like to be there with you."

"I know. Let's just wait until the results are in. I promise to call you as soon as I know something. Now, I think since Brandon is sleeping I'm going to go to the cafeteria to get something to eat. You take care and I'll be in touch. Bye."

I went back to the room and looked at Brandon and he was fast asleep. I think the medicine in his IV was helping him to rest.

I turned and was about to open the door, when he opened his eyes and said, "Are you going home for the night?"

"No. I'm just going to get something to eat. Your parents are on their way. By the time I finish eating they should be here. You rest, I'll be right back."

Just like a little boy, he closed his eyes. I went to the cafeteria and looked around. My appetite was gone, but I was starting to feel weak. I bought a sandwich and a cup of soup. I went over to the table near the door to eat. The moment I sat down and bowed my head for prayer, the tears started flowing uncontrollably down my face. I kept trying to tell myself that I had to be strong for Brandon.

I was able to eat most of my sandwich and all the soup. I went to put my trash in the waste basket. I walked out into the hall and looked both ways. For the life of me I couldn't remember which way to Brandon's room. I made a left turn and started walking down the long hall. I kept walking until I found a chapel. I went inside and took a seat. I prayed and prayed asking God to please heal Brandon's body. I prayed so hard, that my words seemed to get caught in my throat. After wiping my tears, I stood to leave. I turned and there was a nun standing near the door.

She gave me such a warm and friendly smile. She said, "I was listening to your words. I want you to know that God heard them too. You have to know that God is too wise to make a mistake. He made your husband's body, he knows all about it. Keep your faith in God and I promise you, everything is going to work out for your good. Your husband will be able to witness about what God has done for him."

"Thank you. I'd better try to find his room. I know I took the elevator down here, but I didn't pay much attention to where I was going. But if I find the elevators, then I'll know to take it to the 5th floor."

"Come with me. I'll show you to the elevators."

While we were walking she was telling me about Jesus. When I got to the elevators, I thanked her again for showing me the way. She looked in my eyes and said, "Let's have a word of prayer before you leave." She held my hands and prayed for Brandon and me. I thanked her once again. When I got on the elevator, a calm feeling came over my body. I knew then that God heard our prayers and that Brandon was going to be all right.

I made it back to Brandon's room. Before I opened the door I could hear Mother Liz's voice. I walked in. She was standing next to the bed holding Brandon's hand. Daddy

Alexander was sitting with a worried look on his face.

He stood and held me in his arms. I tried to fight back the tears, but they seemed to start flowing more and more down my face. When I was able to get myself together, I dried them and walked over to give Mother Liz a hug. As she turned to hug me, she started crying. This was new to me to see her so fragile. I stood there holding her in my arms and kept telling her that it would to be all right.

Mother Liz and Daddy Alexander stayed in the room for a few hours. I told Brandon that I was going to get them something to eat, and then get them settled in our house. I also said that I was going to pack my overnight bag and come back. He was cute as he told me to take my time—he wasn't going anywhere soon.

We left the hospital and were on our way to get some takeout food. Mother Liz didn't feel like eating, but Daddy Alexander said it had been hours since she had eaten. I knew they were tired from the flight, so I had them to follow me to the house.

After they were inside, I called the soul food restaurant near our house. I knew Mother Liz wouldn't turn down BBQ ribs, so I ordered two meals. I went to the kitchen to clear the mess I left from breakfast. The tray with the one red rose was still sitting on the counter. It brought tears in my eyes. I was so happy this morning making breakfast for Brandon. I wanted him to be served in bed. No way could I have ever imagined anything like this happening. This just goes to show me, I never know what lies ahead.

After picking up their dinners and making sure they were comfortable, it was time to get back to the hospital to be with Brandon. When I arrived in his room, a cot, pillow and blanket were waiting for me. Brandon didn't feel like doing much talking so I just got myself ready to lie down on the cot. It seemed as though each time I would fall to sleep, a nurse would come in to check his vital signs. I tried pulling the covers over my head to dim the light, but it didn't seem to help.

Finally! Morning arrived and I felt like I hadn't slept at all. The shift changed and another nurse came in. She introduced herself to us. She then started asking Brandon some questions. I knew this was a good time for me to head to the bathroom to freshen up. When I came out there were two doctors at his bed.

The first doctor introduced himself as Dr. Chen. The other doctor said his name was Dr. Hammond. I shook hands with each of them. Dr. Chen started looking at Brandon's chart, while Dr. Hammond did all the talking. He said, "Brandon is scheduled for a biopsy this morning. He will be awake during this procedure. We will just numb the area. He'll feel pressure but no pain."

I asked, "When will he get to go home?"

Dr. Hammond said, "We will keep him tonight. We'll be closely watching him for complications."

"Complications? Like what?"

"Like blood clots. We don't want him to move, he has to be very still."

I walked over and stood next to Brandon's bed. I looked at him and said, "Your parents will be here any minute. I'll tell them what I've learned from the doctors."

The nurse came in and said it was time for them to get

Brandon ready. She told me how to get to the waiting room. I looked at the paper she gave me. It said for me to sign in at the waiting area. If I needed to leave, sign out and let the nurse sitting at the desk know where I would be and leave my cell phone number with her. I kissed Brandon on his forehead and told him that I would be waiting. He nodded his head and closed his eyes.

I walked out whispering a prayer. I kept asking Him to please guide the doctor's hands and to take care of Brandon while he was in their care.

I pulled my small black Bible out of my purse to read a few scriptures on faith and healing. My eyes were buried in the pages, when I heard, "There she is." I looked up and it was Brandon's parents. Mother Liz was dressed in a white linen short-sleeved pantsuit. She always looks as if she's doing a photo shoot for a magazine. Daddy Alexander had on a pair of brown pants with a light and dark stripped shirt.

Mother Liz walked over and kissed me on the cheek. She said, "How was Brandon this morning?"

"He really didn't do much talking. I met two of his doctors. They explained that the procedure won't take too long. He will be awake during it. They will numb the area so it won't be painful. The doctor said he'll only feel some pressure."

Daddy Alexander was now sitting next to me. He said, "I'm sure they're going to keep him overnight, to make sure he doesn't form any blood clots."

"The doctor said they would keep him overnight. Mother Liz, did you eat anything for breakfast?"

"Yes. We both had a bagel, coffee and juice."

"I had some breakfast meat in the refrigerator. You didn't

want any of that?"

"No. Since we can't take our medicine on an empty stomach, the bagel was more than enough. By the way, we heard from Lynda this morning. She wants to fly here to be with you and Brandon. I told her to wait—that we were here and we would keep her posted on his condition."

We continued to sit in the waiting room. I called my parents to give them the update on Brandon. Mother Liz spoke with Mom. She kept asking how Brianna was doing. When they hung up, Mother Liz said Mom and Dad would be over tonight, so they could visit with Brianna.

Finally, Dr. Hammond came to see us. I introduced him to Mother Liz and Daddy Alexander. He took us to the conference room and explained that they would be watching Brandon overnight. If he did well, then the plan would be to release him late the next afternoon.

I said to Dr. Hammond, "When he gets home does he have any stipulations?"

He said, "Yes, I want him to get plenty of rest and not pick up anything heavier than ten pounds."

"Ten pounds? Then he can't lift our little girl."

"No. Not right away. Also, he has to watch his sodium intake. Salt will elevate his blood pressure."

"Thanks, Dr. Hammond. I'll pass this information to Brandon. We'll wait here until we can visit with him."

"Brandon won't be happy when I tell him that the doctor said for him to just rest. He's used to seeing people and moving around."

Mother Liz, pointed one of her well manicured fingers in the air and said, "He'll have to listen. We're in town and will make sure he does just what the doctor ordered!"

We sat in the waiting room talking and eating snacks until it was time to visit with Brandon. When we walked in the room, he was asleep. Mother Liz called his name. He slowly opened his eyes, but you could tell he was so tired because he just closed them. We continued our visit for about fifteen minutes, when the nurse came in and asked if we could go out for a minute.

I told Mother Liz that I needed to be in the office tomorrow for an important meeting with my dad and some of the board members. She took me by surprise because she said for me stay home tonight and get a good night sleep so I could be fresh and alert for the meeting. I then asked her what about Brandon? What will happen if they decide to release him in the morning while I'm at work? She said she and Daddy Alexander would get up early and come to the hospital and sit until he's released.

I leaned over and kissed Brandon softly on the lips. He never even moved, so I knew he was tired and would probably sleep until one of the nurses comes in to examine him.

Chapter Thirty

Good Morning, Holy Spirit. I feel like today, God isn't going to let anything happen that He and I can't handle together. I have on a short-sleeved navy and white silk skirt suit. It's hot, but I need to look professional at the board meeting. I went to the kitchen for a glass of orange juice, when I thought I saw the light on. It was! Mother Liz was taking out pots to cook. I said, "Good morning."

She turned around as if she was lost in thought. She looked me up and down and then said, "Hi Linda, you look very nice this morning. I want you not to worry about Brandon, his father and I will be right there by his side. You take care of the business and we'll take care of our son."

She was sounding concerned until she said, "our son." All she had to say was, "Brandon." "Mother Liz my mother said she'll bring Brianna home this evening. I told her I'll be working at home until Brandon is back to work. I'll be able to keep Brianna with us. I know Brandon would be happy seeing her every day."

"I'll be here for another week or so. You can work in your office and we'll take care of Brianna and Brandon. Now you go on so you won't be late."

"Okay, I'll call to check on Brandon. Thanks, Mother Liz."

"You don't have to thank me for taking care of my own son and grandchild."

I left. It was too early for a disagreement.

When I arrived at work, someone had placed a large "welcome back" banner over my office door. As I was preparing for the meeting a couple of the staff members asked if I would go to the large break room with them. I followed them and when I got in there, it was full of co-workers. They were eating Danishes and drinking flavored coffee. One of them started yelling for me to give a speech!

I said. "First of all, I would like to thank everyone for the warm welcome. It's good to be back among friends. I have kept in touch with my secretary, but even she doesn't know what I'm about to say. My husband, Brandon, is in the hospital. They are doing some tests, but the doctor thinks he's suffering from kidney failure."

The room went from complete quietness to a lot of questions. I said, "Please understand that I desire your prayers and I will be back working from home until he's able to return to work. One good thing is we have a computer and a telephone, so I'll still be keeping up with things. Again, thanks for the Danishes and the warm welcome. Now, I'll have one of those sugar coated donuts and a cup of that hazelnut smelling coffee before our meeting."

After getting my donut and coffee, some people returned to their offices, while others stood around asking if there was anything they could do to help me. I started thinking about Brandon, so it was hard fighting back the tears. I thanked them again and left for my office.

Dad emailed that the meeting time has been changed to noon, and lunch would be served. This was great because it gave me time to go over my presentation again.

I was so caught up in my work that I didn't hear my secretary calling me. I happened to look up. She was standing in my doorway about to knock. She just wanted me to know that I had 15 minutes before I needed to be in the conference room.

I thanked her and hurried to the restroom to freshen my makeup. When I came back I checked to see if the light was on my phone. I was hoping to hear from Mother Liz or the hospital. Since I didn't hear from her I thought I would call her to check up on Brandon.

Mother Liz answered Brandon's phone. "Hello. Linda is this you?"

"Yes. I'm on my way to a meeting and just wanted to check on Brandon."

"He's doing better and now he's reaching for the telephone."

"Linda. How was your first day back?"

"Nice. They welcomed me back with a light reception. I'm on my way to a meeting, but wanted to hear how you were doing first."

"I'm doing okay. I just want out of here. Now I know how my patients feel."

He was lightly laughing, but I knew he really did want to go home. "Baby, I have to make this meeting. I'll call you later."

"No. You'll see me at home. Love you!"

"Brandon. I love you too. Bye."

The meeting dragged on for four hours. After my presentation, my mind was really on how Brandon was doing. I kept looking at my watch and saying to myself, *when would this be over?* Finally it was. I stayed around long enough to thank everyone and then I was off to my office. When I got inside there was a note saying Brandon was discharged and was taken home by his parents.

I gathered my things and told my secretary not to worry my father, but to let him know that I'm gone for the day. Also would she please tell him that Brandon has been discharged and for Dad to come over after he left for the day.

I went to the grocery for some steaks to put on the grill for dinner. I made sure to get enough for Mom and Dad. When I got home, Mom's car was in the driveway. I walked through the garage headed for the kitchen. After putting my bags down, I went to the family room but no one was there. I walked outside and there sitting was Mother Liz, Daddy Alexander, Mom and Brianna.

Brianna was bouncing up and down on Daddy Alexander's knee. Mother Liz had her well manicured nails around a crystal glass of wine. Mom was sitting there with a bottle of water. I said, "Hi everyone. Where's Brandon?"

His mother said, "He's in bed. He didn't feel like sitting out here. He said it was too hot."

I went over to kiss Brianna. I said, "I'll be back. I'm going to check on Brandon, change my clothes, and then get our steaks ready for the grill."

Mom said, "Why don't you spend time with Brandon while I get dinner ready." She then looked at Mother Liz and asked if she wanted to help?"

Mother Liz, said, "I'll come in to get another glass of wine, then I'll stay out here and keep Brianna's company."

I looked at Mom and she just turned around and followed me to the kitchen.

After I showed Mom everything I bought, she started marinating the steaks. She said after she washed the vegetables for the grill, she would toss a salad. She kept telling me to go on, she knew where everything was.

I went to the bedroom, looked in and there was Brandon fast asleep. I quietly started undressing. He looked over and said, "Hi."

I walked over and held him in my arms and said, "Hi, yourself, it sure is good having you home."

"It's good to be home. I'm just a little tired. I have been getting so many calls. I told Mother to just let the answering machine get them."

"I bought some steaks. Do you feel like eating?"

"Yes! The doctor increased my prednisone. This medicine makes water taste good. Hey, I forgot to tell you. I heard from Lynda today. She and Carlos are thinking about coming here soon for a weekend. I told her it's okay with me. I'd love to see them and hear all about their cruise."

I finished changing my clothes and tried to get Brandon to leave the bedroom and just sit in the family room, but he didn't feel like it. He did promise to sit at the table with us.

When I went out back to help, Mom was turning the steaks. She wanted to know how to cook them. I told her to completely cook Brandon's and mine all the way done. She wanted to know if Brandon would be joining us for dinner and I said yes.

I went inside to set the table for dinner. Mom had grilled the vegetables and they were in the oven on low. I put the large bowl of garden salad with dressing on the table first and the vegetables in a serving bowl. Each potato with butter was covered in foil and on a serving tray.

Mom had a large pitcher of lemonade garnished with lemon slices floating on top. Just as I finished setting the table, I heard the back door opening.

"Looks like I'm just in time."

"Hi, Dad, you are. Everyone's out back, but I'm ready to call them to dinner. I know. You go and get them while I get Brandon. Oh Dad. The meeting went very well today."

"I thought you nailed them with your presentation. Good job!"

"Thanks."

I went back to get Brandon to eat. He wasn't in the bed. My heart almost stopped! I was thinking *Oh God no! Not again.* I called out to him. He was coming out the bathroom.

He looked at the strange look on my face and said, "I bet you thought I was on the floor again."

"I sure did. Come on, dinner is ready."

Chapter Thirty One

Two weeks went by and every day seemed to be an adventure. Lynda called to say she had some important work at the firm and couldn't come until next weekend. That was all right with us because her parents were still at our house. Mother Liz said since Brandon was doing better, she made reservations for them to leave Monday. I was so happy when she said that. I had been counting the days.

Brandon had been eating but his food didn't seem to give him any energy. All he wanted to do was spend time with Brianna, and sleep. When he wasn't in bed sleeping I found him sitting with his laptop typing. I thought *this is how he keeps up with what's going on with his patients.*

Mother Liz said they were going out for the day. I was happy because all she had done was treat Brandon like he's a child. Every time I tried to say something, she bit my head off. I looked at the calendar on my desk to make sure that today is Friday. Three more days, then just maybe my house can get back in order.

Essie came over to do her weekly cleaning. I was able to get Brandon to sit in the family room, while she cleaned our bedroom. I turned on the TV and tried to make him comfortable, but he wasn't interested in the TV.

I went in our room to talk with Essie. She had her headphones on. She was just working away. I tapped her on the shoulder. She jumped about two inches off the floor. She turned to me and said, "Linda, I was just listening to a book on tape. I was supposed to have read it, but ran out of time. I thought the best way to get it read was to just listen to it. My book club will be discussing this book."

"Is it a good book?"

"Yes."

"Lately, I've been so busy trying to work, take care of Brianna, and Brandon. I've forgotten how to sit and read a good book."

"What are you doing tomorrow?"

"Tomorrow is Saturday. I don't have any special plans. I wish I could just take a long drive to clear my head."

"Why don't you either meet me at our local bookstore or let me pick you up. You could meet some of my book club members. We will be discussing our latest book over lunch."

"Wow! That sounds good. Before you leave, write down which bookstore and the location. If I'm available I'll meet you there."

"Linda you need to get away. Brandon's parents are here. Let them spend the day with him while you take a break."

"I'll let you know. Thanks again for inviting me."

Essie finished cleaning and left the information on the counter about the bookstore. Brandon's parents came in. Mother Liz had a couple bottles of wine. She also had some desserts for dinner. Brandon was back in the bed, but this time he had the TV on. Brianna was asleep so this gave me a chance to get dinner ready.

Mother Liz spent some time in the back talking with Brandon. She came to the kitchen to get another glass of wine. She looked at the note on the counter and said, "Is this an invitation for you tomorrow?"

"Yes. I've been invited to a book discussion. I was thinking about seeing if my mother would keep Brianna while I go and be with the ladies for a little while."

"Your mother doesn't have to keep Brianna. We're here, let her stay with us. We'll take care of her and Brandon. I think you should get out for a few hours with the girls."

"Mother Liz, do you really mean it?"

"I wouldn't have said it if I didn't."

I found myself hugging her all while I was saying, "Oh, thank you!"

Dinner was good and so was the conversation. Brandon's parents laughed and talked about their day. Brandon didn't feel like leaving the bed, so he ate in our room on a TV tray. He really seemed like he was slipping into depression. Lately we haven't even had a decent conversation. If I say it looks like it's going to rain, he'll then say something smart. This is not like him at all. I think it's the medicine he's taking. I'm going to call his doctor tomorrow to see if he could see Brandon next week.

Today is Saturday and I'm so happy to be meeting Essie's friends. I spent most of the morning taking care of Brianna and Brandon. When it was time to get ready to go, I must have gotten dressed in record time. I'm feeling pretty good.

I asked Brandon if he needed anything before I left and, he said no, he was doing all right. I went to the family room where Mother Liz was playing with Brianna. I told her that I was on my way to the bookstore. She was nice enough to tell me not to hurry back to enjoy my day with the girls.

When I arrived at the bookstore, there wasn't a parking spot in sight. I had to park across the street which caused me to have to walk a distance. As I got closer to the store, there was a long line of people. I felt like going back home. I said to myself, *it's too hot to be standing in a long line.* But then I heard my name being called. I started walking towards the sound and saw it was Essie waving for me to come up near the front of the line.

I started walking fast. I really didn't want anyone to yell at me for cutting the line. When I got to where she was, she hugged me and said, "Linda, I'm so happy you came." She then started pointing at the six ladies that were in the front of her. She introduced me to them. I said it was nice meeting them.

We were almost to the table when Essie started talking, she was so excited. She asked me. "Have you ever met a real best-selling author before?"

Before I could answer, she started again. "Her name is Michelle Larks and she has written several books. I've met her in the past and she is so nice. You see this line of people don't you? Well, they wouldn't be here if the sister couldn't write. Her stories are wonderful. When we get up to meet her, you'll see. She treats you like she's an old friend."

"What book are we buying today?"

"Her latest book is titled *Keeping Misery Company.* It received great reviews. I wouldn't be surprised if she's asked to make it into a movie."

I just stood there thinking about the title of the book. It reminded me of Brandon. Lately, I find myself keeping misery company and he's misery.

It was my time to meet the author. I said, "Hello. My name is Linda. Please autograph it to me."

She gave me a big friendly smile and said, "I thank you for coming in all this hot weather just for me. Also, sign my guest book so you'll receive my monthly newsletter."

I said, "I will. Thank you for signing my book."

She stood and gave me a big hug and thanked me again.

I walked away feeling appreciated. I didn't know we could touch her, since her bodyguard was standing next to the table.

When it was time for Essie to meet the author, she started talking like she was at the end of the line. She told her that she was the president of her book club. She was on her mailing list and that this was not her first time meeting her. She had the author to sign her copies. Essie took her camera out of her purse and gave it to the bodyguard. He looked at Ms. Lark to see if it was okay. She said yes, so he took the picture. Essie walked away feeling like they were now best friends.

One of the ladies said that since she was driving an SUV, some of the ladies should ride with her and some with Essie. By doing this, we wouldn't have to take all the cars to the restaurant.

Two of the ladies and I walked over to ride with Essie. Essie told the other driver to follow her. She said we were going to a great seafood restaurant that wasn't too far away.

When we arrived, there weren't any open parking places. After circling the building twice, she found a spot behind the building. She parked and we went in to see if we could have a small banquet room.

Essie told the manager that we wanted to have a book discussion. She also told him there were eight of us. He understood and asked us to follow him to the room in the back. I waited for the other ladies, so they would know where we were sitting.

That day turned out to be just what I needed! The conversation about the book was good and the ladies put me in the mood of wanting to go right home, crack open my book and start reading.

The food was excellent! And the ladies made me feel as if I was a member. I told them that as soon as I got my life back on track, that I would like to be considered a member of their book club. Essie said they met the second Saturday of each month at a different member's house.

Riding back to my car, I kept thanking Essie for inviting me to meet such nice, friendly ladies. I told her she was right! I needed to get away from the house. I smiled at myself because I didn't know what was facing me when I got home, but I did know that I was leaving there feeling like a brand new woman.

As I was driving up to the house, the first thing I noticed was that Mother Liz's rental car wasn't in the driveway. I hoped and prayed nothing had happened to Brandon. I pulled in the garage and hurried in to make sure everything was all right. I walked in the kitchen, and had put my book on the counter, when the aroma of something good hit my nostrils. I stopped to breathe in the flavor. Then I heard a faint voice, so I followed the sound to the family room.

I looked in and saw Mother Liz with a glass of red wine in her right hand and the cordless telephone in her left. As I was about to enter to let her know that I was back, I heard her laugh and say, "Olivia, I'm so happy you and Brandon have been keeping in touch emailing each other. I know if you could be here you would." Then I heard her say, "That would be nice. I know Brandon would love to see you. I'll let him know your plans."

Olivia? The times I saw him on his laptop I was thinking that he was communicating with some of the doctors in his practice, but from what I just heard I guess he was talking to Olivia. I quietly backed out into the hall before she saw me. I went to the bedroom to check on Brandon. I looked in and he was holding Brianna in his arms, while they both slept.

I went to the kitchen to get something cold to drink, and closed the refrigerator, when Mother Liz walked in. She said, "Why Linda, I didn't hear you come in."

I looked at her and waited before answering. I wanted so badly to say, I've been here long enough to hear the conversation you had with Olivia." Instead, I said, "I haven't been here that long. I was in the back checking on Brandon and Brianna."

"You didn't wake them did you?"

"No. I peeked in and then walked out. Where is Daddy Alexander?"

"Your father invited him to a game of golf at the country club. He said your mother had things to do and one of them was visiting your grandmother. Did you have a good time with the girls?"

"Yes. They had a book discussion while we ate lunch. I do

hope when Brandon is back on his feet, that I can join their book club."

"I think that would be nice. Oh! You had two calls from your friends in Florida. They asked about Brandon. They said the three of you have been keeping in touch by email. You know that is the "going thing" now. Everyone's emailing!"

I wanted to say, "Yes I know, but instead I said, "I'll call them later. What's in the oven, that smells so good?"

She said, "It's only a baked beef and noodles casserole. I'm going to serve it with fresh green beans, sliced tomatoes, onions and dinner rolls."

"It sure does smell good. Thank you for going to all of this trouble to make dinner for us."

"It's no trouble at all. I'll be leaving so I made plenty. You can freeze some and have it another time."

"I'm going to call my friends to tell them all about my day. If you need me I'll be in my office."

"I won't need you. I have everything under control. I think I'll pour another glass of wine and go back in the family room to watch a little TV."

I passed the bedroom for one more look to make sure Brandon was all right. Brianna was still asleep, but Brandon was sitting on the side of the bed with the telephone up to his ear. He had his back to me, so I stood to listen.

He said, "Pastor I won't be at church tomorrow and I thank you for praying with me. I feel like this is the time in my life that I should be enjoying my wife and baby, but here I am in bed ill with no energy."

He wiped his eyes and started talking again. I heard all I needed to hear, so I continued down the hall to my office.

I wanted to call Monica and Christa, but I didn't feel like talking to them. I felt like I needed to spend some time with God. I took out my Bible and started reading. When I finished, my next step would be to pray. Only God can take us through this storm.

Chapter Thirty Two

On Monday Brandon's parents had an early flight. They didn't want any breakfast, but they did have prayer with us before going to the airport. They called later to let me know that they returned the rental car and had breakfast at the airport. I told them that Brandon didn't eat and that I was going to call his doctor to make an appointment.

Mother Liz kept asking if I needed her to stay a little longer, I told her no. If Brandon's condition changed in any way, I would call them immediately. My Mom took Brianna home last night because she knew that I was going to try to get Brandon in to see the doctor today.

I took Brandon a small glass of orange juice because I wanted him to have something in his stomach. He started to drink some, but wasn't able to keep it down. He threw up all over himself and the bed.

As I gathered the waste basket and towels to help him, I looked at him. He looked so fragile. Even his eyes looked as though they were changing colors, like they were yellowing.

After I got him all cleaned up and dressed, I called the doctor's office. The receptionist said Dr. Hammond was at the hospital and wouldn't be in until late morning. I gave her my name and said that I was on my way to the emergency room with Brandon.

Brandon didn't want to go. He kept saying he just needed to rest. I told him either he could let me drive him or I was going to call an ambulance. He put his arms around my neck and we slowly walked to the car.

When we got to the hospital, the admitting nurse hurried out with a wheelchair to help us inside. She remembered us and took Brandon to a room while I parked the car.

After I came in, she told me which room Brandon was in. When I got back there, the techs were drawing blood. Dr. Hammond came in and said, he was putting a rush on the blood results. He called me in the hall.

He said, "I didn't want Brandon to hear me, but from the way he looks, I'm sure he is going to have to start dialysis immediately! He'll probably be on a schedule of Monday, Wednesday, and Friday."

I felt like fainting while Dr. Hammond was talking. I just stood there frozen, but my mind was saying Jesus! Jesus! Jesus!

I said, "Dr. Hammond, we have a little girl, and I don't want to lose my husband. Can I be typed to see if my kidney would be a match for him?"

"Linda, is this something you and Brandon have discussed? The reason I'm asking is because donors seem to have a hard time with the surgery. The recipient body is either going to accept the kidney with the help of medications or reject it. Do you think Brandon would want to subject you to this kind of surgery?"

"No, we never discussed this, but I just can't see a gifted

doctor like Brandon sitting around waiting every other day for dialysis."

"Does he have any siblings?"

"He has only one sister and knowing Brandon, he wouldn't want her to risk her kidneys to give him one. What if she and her husband would want to have more children and something happens to the one she had left. Then she would have to be on dialysis."

"Ask Brandon if he would like to be put on the transplant list. Then he won't have to ask anyone. We'll keep his information on file and if a cadaver becomes available, we will use that person's kidney."

"But what are the chances of someone dead with the same blood type and everything else you need to match that person with Brandon?"

"It's just the chance we take. Not all people are donors, but the ones who are, we try to use their parts when they die. Linda, I'm sure either he has to have a transplant or dialysis."

Another nurse came to say that the lab wanted to speak with Dr. Hammond. He excused himself and I went back in the room to be with Brandon.

"Linda, It's bad isn't it?"

"No. Not really."

"Linda, I'm a doctor and when we take a family member to the hallway, we don't want to upset the patient. Now give it to me straight."

"Dr. Hammond said he is waiting for your blood work. He's pretty sure you'll have to go on dialysis starting today. Brandon, I would like to have my blood drawn to see if I'm a match."

"No. I can't put you through that."

"Then what are you going to do?"

"I'm going to stay strong and stay prayerful that God will see me through this."

"Brandon you've gone to school to be a doctor and you're a good one at that. I just can't let you give up your career. You can't work and take dialysis three times a week."

"I know. Like I said, we need to not worry. Worrying isn't going to solve anything. Now I need you to go out and call my sister. And when my parents are home, please call them for me."

"I'll do just that."

I kissed him on his forehead and walked out. His eyes were filling up with tears and I knew he didn't want me to see him crying.

I called my mother and the phone rang and rang, she finally answered. "Hello, hello."

"Mom this is Linda. I'm at the hospital with Brandon."

"Oh my God! Has he turned for the worse?"

"Yes. His doctor is thinking that he will need dialysis today."

"Today? Did his parents have a direct flight?"

"No. They have a layover."

"Then you should try calling them. Maybe they can take a flight back here."

"Good idea. I'll call you later."

I dialed Mother Liz's cell and she picked up. "Mother Liz this is Linda and we are at the hospital."

"Hospital! Is Brandon all right?"

"They took some blood, but the doctor said he feels like

Brandon will have to have dialysis today."

"I was going to call you because our plane had engine trouble, so we are sitting here waiting for them to either repair it or send another plane. God works in mysterious ways. We're going to get our luggage, rent a car and we'll meet you at the hospital."

"Oh thank you!"

I called my mother to let her know that Brandon's parents were still in town at the airport. She wanted to cancel her plans for today and come out to sit with me, but I told her to keep her plans.

I called Brandon's sister to let her know how he was doing. She said she was going to call Carlos and have him meet her at home immediately. She said they would be on the next flight out of Chicago.

I was happy they were coming. I knew when Brandon saw her, he would know how his family is concerned. I had to make one more important call.

"Hello. Brenda, this is Linda Alexander, is Pastor in?"

"No. he left for Louisville this morning. It's time for the annual conference. He won't be back until late Saturday. Is there anything I can help you with?"

"Brandon isn't doing well at all. In fact, I'm calling you from the hospital."

"Hospital? I knew he was ill because his name is on our prayer list and we all prayed for him Wednesday night. Do you want to speak with Minister Carolyn Drane?"

"Yes."

"Wait here while I get her to the phone."

"Hello. Linda, this is Minister Carolyn. Brenda just told

me that Brandon is in the hospital. I know he's probably in the one near your house."

"Yes."

"I'll be right there, but first, let's have prayer. You know God is still in the blessing business and I want you to know that there is nothing too hard for God."

She prayed and prayed. When she finished, I dried my eyes and told her that I would meet her in the emergency waiting room.

I went back to Brandon. This time there were three doctors. They introduced themselves. Dr. Hammond said Brandon's blood work was read by all three doctors and he was correct. Brandon had to be admitted and would be given his first dialysis treatment today.

I told Brandon that his parents were still in town and on their way to the hospital. And that Lynda and Carlos would be here sometime today. Also, that I had called the church to get our pastor to come to the hospital to have prayer with us, but he was out of town and I was able to reach one of our other ministers on staff. He wanted to know who, and I told him it was Minister Carolyn Drane. He smiled because he liked her and was happy that she was going to pray with us. I told him I'd better check the waiting room to see if she has arrived.

When I got to the waiting room Minister Carolyn was sitting and reading her Bible. I walked over and sat in the empty seat next to her. She looked over and smiled. She said, "Honey, I promise you, things aren't always what they seem. You have got to have faith in God. This is only a test. After I've prayed with Brandon, I'll write down some scriptures on faith. I want you to read them and meditate on them."

I hugged her and my tears started flowing. She held me in her arms, saying all the while to trust God. She said, "Linda, God has a kidney waiting for Brandon. We don't know when it will arrive or who will be the donor, but I have enough faith in God that He's going to supply Brandon with one."

Wiping my eyes, I whispered, "I believe what you're saying, because I too have faith and believe in the power of God."

Minister Carolyn and I walked in the room. Brandon looked up and smiled at her. She held his hand and prayed with us. When she finished, Brandon thanked her. Then a nurse came in and asked us to leave so they could prep Brandon for his treatment. We were told that it was going to take four hours. Minister Carolyn wanted to sit with me, but I told her that I wouldn't be alone, that Brandon's parents were on their way and so were his sister and brother-in-law.

But she wouldn't take no for an answer. We walked to the waiting room and she said she was going to sit with me until his parents arrived. When we got to the waiting room I signed in and called Mother Liz to tell her where to meet me.

I found myself staring at the large clock on the wall. It looked as though the hands were not moving. The other people in the waiting area were either looking at TV or talking. I kept looking at the door waiting for Mother Liz and Daddy Alexander to arrive. Minister Carolyn was nice enough to get us a cold drink from the vending machine. I wasn't hungry but I sure was thirsty. She was God-sent to me. She was talking so much about life and how people can act that I actually found myself laughing.

Finally, Brandon's parents came in. I introduced them to Minister Carolyn and I told them that she was one of the Ministers on staff at our church. Mother Liz said it was nice of her to come out and sit with me. I told them by now Brandon was getting his first treatment. Mother Liz wanted to know if he knew that they were still in town. I told her yes and told her that Lynda and Carlos would also be here sometime today.

As Minister Carolyn was leaving she said to please call if I needed her. I thanked her again as we walked to the elevator just outside of the waiting area.

We sat a little longer, until Daddy Alexander said his stomach was making all sorts of noise. Mother Liz said she could use a meal too, but didn't want to leave just in case Brandon's treatment was over and he was asking for them. I had to explain to her that I had given them my cell phone number and it was okay to sign out. If they needed me, they would call.

We went to the cafeteria to get some soup and sandwiches. We sat and ate. There was little conversation between us, probably because we were all really hungry.

My cell phone rang. It was Lynda. She said they were in the parking lot and needed to know where we were. I gave her instructions to the cafeteria and said we would be sitting there waiting for them.

When they arrived it was only Lynda and Carlos. Mother Liz shouted in a loud tone, "Where is the baby?"

Lynda said, "With our babysitter. Carlos and I talked it over and thought since we would be back and forth to the hospital visiting with Brandon, this would be no place for a young child."

Mother Liz said, "I guess since you put it like that, you're right. I just wanted to see my little man."

Carlos who usually doesn't say much said, "You'll just have to come to Chicago and visit with him."

Mother Liz smiled and said, "Is that an invitation?"

Carlos said, "You don't need an invitation to visit us! You're always welcome."

Lynda and Carlos went to get something to eat. When they returned, she took some pictures from her purse to show us how much fun they had on their cruise. Little Carlos was all smiles on each picture. He was especially happy in the ones where he was in the swimming pool.

We all were enjoying the pictures when Mother Liz had to spoil it. She started asking Lynda what was she wearing in some of the pictures.

Chapter Thirty Three

We were sitting and talking when my cell phone rang. It was the nurse asking us to return to the waiting area because Brandon's doctor would like to meet with us.

No sooner had we arrived when the nurse pointed to the conference room. She said the doctor would be there any minute. We went in and waited, and when Dr. Hammond came in, I introduced him to Brandon's sister, Lynda, and her husband, Carlos. He shook their hands and took a seat.

He said, "Brandon did real well with his first treatment. He is really tired. We tried to feed him but he wasn't able to keep his food down. He is scheduled for another treatment Wednesday and another one Friday."

Before I could say anything, his sister said, "Dr. Hammond my brother is a great physician. I know he can't practice medicine in this condition and I would hate to see him sit around and practically die! I'm saying "die" because he loves caring for people. I would like you to test my blood to see if I'm a match for him to receive one of my kidneys."

Dr. Hammond said, "It's not a problem to write you an order to have your blood drawn and tested, but you first need to talk this over with Brandon. Not today, but maybe tomorrow."

I said, "Dr. Hammond, do you mean we can't see him now?"

"You can see him, but he's very weak. He probably won't even remember you being here. My suggestion is that you have a short visit, then come back tomorrow around noon. That way he would have eaten a little breakfast and should feel a lot stronger."

We all shook Dr. Hammond's hand and thanked him for all he had done for Brandon. He told us to follow him to his room. I looked over at his sister, she was drying her tears. Daddy Alexander reached out and held her in his arms. He told her she had to be strong for Brandon and that everything was going to be all right.

When we got to his room, Brandon was sleeping. Mother Liz rushed to his side and kissed him on the cheek, and whispered something in his ear. Brandon opened his eyes and a single tear fell from his left eye.

I walked over and kissed him on the lips and told him that we all were there—even Lynda. She walked over and held his hand. She tried to keep from crying. She leaned down and kissed him on his forehead and said, "Brandon I'm here for you and I mean that. If you need one of my kidneys, just say the word and it's yours."

Brandon turned and looked toward Daddy Alexander and Carlos and smiled. He cleared his throat to speak. He said, "It sure is good seeing all of you. I want you to know that I refuse to let this defeat me. I know God has a plan for my life and it isn't coming here three times a week for a treatment."

The tears started to flow down all of our faces. There wasn't a dry eye in the room. Daddy Alexander said, "You're right Brandon, you have to keep the faith. I want you to know that your mother and I will be here with you. We promise to see you through this ordeal."

Lynda said, "That goes for me too. I can't stay because we left little Carlos with his sitter, but you will always be in my prayers. Also, I'm just a phone call away."

Mother Liz glanced at the clock on the wall. She said, "We've been here quite a while and the doctor said he need his rest. Brandon, we'll be back tomorrow."

He looked over at Lynda and said, "You too?"

Lynda took a deep breath before answering. She said, "Carlos and I will be back tomorrow. Now you go on and rest as much as you can."

I kissed him again. He closed his eyes as we quietly left the room. When we got in the hall Mother Liz said she wanted to call Olivia to update her on his condition. I told her that was a good idea I'm sure she would want to know how he's doing.

Brandon stayed in the hospital for one more treatment and was released. He tried to be strong because his sister and parents were there. But that all changed when it was just the two of us. Brandon would come home from his treatments tired and short tempered. I tried to not let it bother me because I knew he was ill. On the days of his treatment, we would have prayer together. Then we would drive Brianna to Mother's. I would either take a book or just sit and talk to him, but most times, he would just close his eyes and act as if I wasn't even there.

Three weeks had gone by. Brandon was still taking his treatments every other day and I was trying to do as much work as I could on those days. His parents and Olivia were calling after each treatment to see how he was feeling. Our pastor and Minister Carolyn had been calling to have prayer with Brandon. Each time it seemed to lift his spirits, but then shortly after he hung up the phone he seemed to fall back into a state of depression.

On Thursday I got up with a prayer on my lips and a song of praise in my heart. I made breakfast for Brandon and demanded that he come to the table to eat. He must have seen that I was getting tired of the pity party he was hosting. Mom kept Brianna overnight so I could get some work done and some much needed rest.

I was putting our plates on the table when Brandon walked in dressed in a short sleeved white shirt and a pair of jeans. I was happy to see he wasn't in his pajamas. I said, "You look nice this morning."

He dropped his head. He then tugged at his jeans to show me how much weight he had lost. He looked up and said, "Linda I'm sorry for all I've put you through. I don't mean to be hateful towards you because I do know that you're doing your very best. You are trying to work from home, take care of Brianna and take me to dialysis three times a week. Please forgive me."

"Brandon. This is new to both of us. You can't help the condition your body is in. I want you to know that when I stood before our minister and God and said I would love you in sickness and in health. I meant every word. I know that if I was ill, you would move heaven and earth to take care of me."

"You're right. Just bear with me again, please forgive me. I know that God is going to heal me in His time. Now let's eat our breakfast before it gets cold."

I hugged him tight before sitting down. My spirit was thanking God for the strength He gave Brandon this morning. He wasn't eating on the side of the bed, but was at the dining room table.

Brandon spent most of the day in the family room on his computer. I kept going in to check on him. He seemed to be having a good day. I called Mom to see when she was going to bring Brianna home. She said they were going to visit Grandmother. Then she was taking her for a stroll in the park. I told her I was going to complete some of my work, then try and get Brandon out of the house.

I must have been caught up in my work because when I looked at the clock two hours had passed. I sat there thinking that I hadn't heard a sound out of Brandon. I got off the computer quickly to check on him.

He had put his laptop on the table in the family room and was curled up on the sofa asleep. I didn't want to disturb him, so I went back to answer some e-mails.

Brandon finally got up. He came to my office and asked if I had anything good to eat. I laughed and asked him what he had a taste for. He wanted a hotdog with plenty of mustard and relish. I had to smile because I knew tomorrow would be his treatment and he wouldn't want to eat any solid foods.

I told him to let me log off and put on my shoes, so we could go out for a nice lunch. I told him that I was in no mood for a hotdog. I wanted a big juicy hamburger with all the fixings. He laughed and so did I. It felt good to see him laugh again.

Just as I was putting on my shoes the phone rang. It was the nurse calling from the hospital. She said for me to bring Brandon immediately, they had a kidney and he was on the list to receive it. I thanked her and ran to the family room yelling. "Brandon, they have a kidney for you! We've got to leave now. That was the hospital calling! Did you hear me?"

Brandon looked up. He then dropped his head, as the tears started to flow down his face. I ran over and held him in my arms and said, "Thank you, God, for this miracle."

Just as we were going out the door the phone rang again. I told Brandon, let's not answer it, let the machine pick it up. He agreed. I went to the kitchen to get the keys off the hook. Brandon was walking out the door when we heard the message.

"This is the nurse, Bonnie Ward. I'm the lady who called you earlier. Please call me back, there has been a misunderstanding. I'll leave my number at the end of this message. Again, please call me before coming to the hospital."

Chapter Thirty Four

Brandon and I stood there looking at the answering machine. He didn't say a word and neither did I. It must have been about two minutes before I said to him. "Brandon I'm going to call the nurse to see what's going on."

Brandon sat down while I made the call. I had to leave a message because she didn't answer. I looked over at Brandon. He was sitting with his head hung low. I didn't know what to say so I just walked over and held him close to me.

The phone rang. I jumped and it seemed as though my heart actually missed a beat. When I answered it, it was the nurse calling. She started the conversation by apologizing for the first call. She explained that she usually works the third shift, but she was filling in for someone.

She told me that it had been busy when the call came in that a kidney was available. She typed in the information and Brandon's name came up. What she didn't know was that another nurse had made contact with a patient whose name was listed before Brandon's. She kept saying she had made a big mistake and hoped that Brandon would understand. She asked me to please tell him that his name was definitely the next on the list. I thanked her for calling and said that I would explain the misunderstanding to Brandon.

Brandon had been sitting there listening to the entire conversation. I was at a loss for words. I just stood there shaking my head. I told him not to give up, there would be another kidney available and that he was next on the list. He surprised me. He stood and said, "let's go out to eat because I'm still hungry." I was surprised. I thought he would have just wanted to go to bed and wait for tomorrow's treatment.

After we ate, Brandon wanted to go by Mom's to see Brianna. I called and they were home, but Brianna was asleep. Mom said she would bring her home later. I tried to lift Brandon's spirits by asking if he wanted to take in a movie, but he didn't feel like it.

We went home and waited for Mom to bring Brianna. Brandon went straight to the bedroom. At lunch he ate, but he was quiet the entire time. I knew he really didn't feel like talking so I went to the family room to call Monica.

It had been a few days since we'd talked. She was happy to hear my voice because our last few conversations were by e-mail. She wanted to know how Brandon was doing and how was I holding up. I told her that I was being kept by the best. That God wasn't going to put any more on me than I could handle.

I started telling her about how happy Brandon and I were earlier today, until we received the call from the hospital. Monica's words went from a soft tone to loud shouting. She was quite upset and said I should get an attorney and sue the pants off that hospital. I told her it was an honest mistake.

She didn't agree, but then she changed the subject. She started laughing for no reason. I asked her, why all the laughter? She wanted to wait until her doctor's appointment, but said she took a home pregnancy test and it was positive. She was going to have a baby. She said this would be the first grandchild for her parents and her in-laws. I asked her if she had told Christa and she said yes, she called her last night after taking the test.

I was so happy for her and her husband. I told her it was a blessing from God. I said that after all of this was behind us, we would come to Jacksonville to see her and all the old neighbors.

We ended the call by praying for each another. She prayed for Brandon and me. I prayed for her and her unborn child.

I went back in the bedroom to check on Brandon. He was sitting up clicking away on this laptop. He told me that Olivia was making plans to visit us this weekend. When I asked how long was she staying, he said she didn't know. She was coming on a one- way ticket. He seemed to be all smiles while telling me this news.

I ended the conversation saying that would be nice and left the room. I walked out talking under my breath, saying *"When were you going to let me know. I'm the one who has to do the cooking for the guest."*

On Friday, after Brandon's last treatment until Monday morning, he seemed to be chipper. I asked him since Olivia would be here in the morning, if it would be okay with him if I left him at the treatment center, while I go to do some grocery shopping. He was already a step ahead of me. He lifted his small bag to show me that he had a book to keep him company.

We rode to the center in silence. I was listening to gospel

music and Brandon was singing along with the artist. I kept my eyes on the road but kept thinking, *how am I going to get through this with Olivia being here?*

After taking the groceries home, I went back to get Brandon. He wasn't too tired and sleepy. He actually held a decent conversation as we drove to Mom's to pick up Brianna.

When we got home, Brandon went to the kitchen to drink some green tea. He said he wasn't hungry, but he did feel like eating a little potato soup. I asked if he wanted me to bring it to the bedroom. He said no, that he would like to eat at the dining room table.

I was thinking *that either Brandon was getting used to these treatments or he was trying to make himself feel like he's handling it. I think he wants to impress Olivia, since she'll be here Monday when he has another treatment.*

Brandon gave it his best shot. He ate and the next thing I knew, he was in the middle of the bed sleeping. I had a large bowl of popcorn in one hand and Brianna in the other. We went to the family room to find a good Lifetime movie.

The next morning sunshine woke me. I looked on the other side of the bed and saw that Brandon was gone. Walking down the hall I looked in the other bedrooms-still no Brandon. I went to the kitchen and there he was, sitting and reading the newspaper, while drinking a glass of orange juice.

This was a sight that I hadn't seen in weeks! He had shaved and wasn't in those cotton shorts and under shirt. He was wearing silk pajamas and looking good. Brianna was swinging in her swing, kicking her legs and smiling. I found myself actually smiling back.

The morning was busy for me. I had to make sure everything was looking nice for our visitor. I even bought a set of towels for her personal use. Brandon noticed how much I was trying because he told me to rest, that Olivia was family. He said I had been moving ever since I got up. I explained that was my duty as the lady of the house, to make sure everything was clean, decent and in order.

Brandon didn't go back to sleep. He got dressed and said he felt like putting some meat on the grill. I almost lost my teeth when he said that! I was so used to him still taking it easy on the day after his treatments.

I wasn't going to crush him since he was feeling pretty good. In fact, I followed him outside to get the patio clean so we could eat out there. He said Olivia's plane would be in around 4:00 p.m. and she should be at the house close to 6:00 p.m.

That would give me plenty of time to get the baked beans, potato salad, garden salad and iced tea ready. I would even have time to marinate the steaks for Brandon. He called inviting my parents to dinner. Mom said she and Dad didn't have any plans and would love to come.

Before I knew it, the door bell rang. I hurried to see if it was Mom and Dad. When I opened the door, it wasn't my parents, but Olivia standing there looking like a million bucks. She was dressed in a yellow linen pantsuit and sporting a new hairdo. She no longer had the long hair, it was now neatly cut short. It actually made her look even younger.

She smiled as I opened the door and gave me a friendly hug. I hugged her back and told her how happy I was to see her. She asked for Brianna and Brandon. I told her they were in the backyard. I showed her to the guestroom and said when she unpacked to please come out back and join us.

Brandon came in and asked if that was Olivia? I told him yes, she was in the room hanging up her things. He rushed past me to see her. I went back outside because he left Brianna alone in her swing.

While I sat there playing with Brianna, they finally both came out. Olivia was smiling and so was Brandon. He was happy to have her in our home. I offered her something to drink. She said Daddy Alexander bragged about my iced tea, so she would like to try it.

I left them outside talking and laughing. It was good seeing Brandon in such a happy mood, even if I wasn't the one who was making him laugh!

Chapter Thirty Five

The weekend went better than I thought. Olivia went to church with Brandon and me. While walking to the car, she remarked how much she enjoyed the service. Brandon made a suggestion that we take Olivia to one of his favorite restaurants. When we pulled up, the parking lot was packed. Brandon let us out at the door, while he looked for a parking space.

Olivia and I went in because it was so hot outside. Just before we sat down, Brandon came through the door. The manager came over to talk with Brandon. He gave me a friendly hug and asked Brandon if Olivia was his sister. Brandon introduced him to Olivia.

The manager was all smiles as he excused himself. Just as the three of us started talking, the manager came back and asked us to follow him to a table that just became available. The atmosphere was nice, the food was good and so was the conversation.

Just before leaving the restaurant, I excused myself to change Brianna's diaper. As the door was closing, I looked behind me and there was Olivia behind me. She asked if it was okay for her to drive Brandon to his treatment in the morning. I told her yes, that would give me time to get caught up on some things.

When we arrived home, Brianna was fast asleep. I took her to the nursery so she'd continue her nap. Olivia went to the guestroom to change clothes. Brandon and I did the same thing.

Most of the night we were in the family room watching TV. Brandon was happy that Olivia was taking him to his treatment. He said not once but twice, how this would give me time to take care of some of my errands.

The next morning, I got up early to prepare a light breakfast for Olivia. Brandon typically didn't eat anything before his treatment. Olivia came to breakfast so we ate and talked a little. Finally, Brandon came in and they left.

Four hours had passed. I spent my time visiting with Mom and running errands. Essie came by the house to do her weekly cleaning. Just as I was driving up to the house, she was leaving. She pulled up next to me.

"Hi. Linda. How's things going today?"

"Hi. Essie. Olivia is in town, you know, she's the friend who lost her parents in a plane crash. Well, she was nice enough to take Brandon for his treatment to give me time to run my errands."

"You've been very busy and I want you to know that I have been praying for you. When I read Psalm 46:1, I always call out your name, so God will give you strength. He said "He is our refuge and strength, a very present help in trouble.""

"Thank you, Essie. No way can I do all of this without God. He's the only one who's keeping me strong. It's getting hard, but I'm giving it all I've got. I know Brandon didn't ask for this illness and I know that if we keep the faith, God will see us through."

"You've got it. Keep the faith! Now I have one more house to clean, but you know if you need me for anything and I mean anything, I'm just a phone call away."

"I know you are and thank you for the offer. I better get Brianna in the house so I can change her diaper and feed her. Thanks again."

After getting Brianna taken care of, she fell asleep in my arms. I lay her down and went to the kitchen to make a light lunch so when Brandon and Olivia came home, Olivia could eat. I know Brandon will only want a bowl of soup and a sandwich. Most times, he wants a grilled sandwich, but this time I've made some chicken salad.

No sooner had I finished chopping up the fruit when I heard the garage door. I reached for the cream of potato soup container that I had bought from the restaurant for Brandon. The door flew open and Brandon looked tired and sleepy. He spoke and went right to the bedroom.

"Olivia, thank you so much for taking him for me. I got a chance to get a lot done today."

"Linda, you don't have to thank me. I wanted to do this because I needed to meet his doctor in person. We needed to talk about Brandon's condition."

"I'll take Brandon his soup and sandwich. I have some chicken salad sandwiches and fresh fruit. Why don't you fix your plate and meet me in the backyard. We can talk out there in private."

"Okay. You take care of Brandon and I'll be waiting for you."

When I got to the bedroom with the tray of food, Brandon was already in his pajamas and fast asleep. I knew he was weak and only wanted to sleep, but I had to wake him so he could have something in his stomach. After calling his name several times, he finally woke. He sat up. I spoon fed him some of the soup. He said it was good and took the spoon from me to feed himself. I sat there while he ate all of the soup. He took a few bites of the sandwich and drank all of the water. He thanked me for the meal and said he needed to rest. I kissed him, picked up his tray and left.

I went in to check on Brianna, she was still sleeping. I grabbed the monitor to take outside, so if she started to cry, I could get her before she disturbed Brandon.

I went into the kitchen to take the tray and fix myself a sandwich and fruit. When I finished, I walked out back. Olivia was sitting there reading the Bible. I thanked her again for taking Brandon. Again, she said it was something she wanted to do. I said my blessing and had started eating when she put the Bible down and said to me.

"Linda, Brandon and I have been friends for a very long time. There isn't anything I wouldn't do for him or you. I wanted to come here for a reason. That reason is I would like to donate one of my kidneys to Brandon."

"Olivia, I'm not the one you should be talking to about this. I also don't think Brandon will let you do this."

"It's no secret that I've been in contact with him and his mother. She gave me Dr. Hammond's telephone number. That's why I wanted to go with him today. I wanted to meet Dr. Hammond in person. I've talk with him about Brandon. Now before you say anything, hear me out. I know due to confidentiality rules he wasn't supposed to tell me anything concerning Brandon's health. He didn't, but he did listen to my suggestion. I had my blood drawn in Massachusetts and the results were faxed to Dr. Hammond. He contacted me to let me know that I just might be a match for Brandon."

"Olivia, he will never let you be a donor."

"I think he would. Especially, when he hears me out. My parents are dead and I don't think I'll ever get married and have a family. Since their death, I have a different outlook on life. Brandon is a great physician and I just don't want him sitting around here waiting for a cadaver's organ. Not when I might be the very one who can help. My interest is going back home to start an innercity clinic to help the poor."

"What do you need from me?"

"I need you to back me up when I talk with Brandon tomorrow."

"Tomorrow?"

"Yes. Tomorrow. I need you to agree with everything I have to say. Dr. Hammond said the sooner we agree, the sooner he could schedule us for the surgery."

"Olivia, I have to say something. When you said you wanted to come here, I didn't know how to handle you. You have always been nice to me, but Mother Liz has expressed that if she had a choice, you would have been her daughter-in-law. This has really intimidated me."

"Linda I don't mean to cut you off, but Mother Liz thinks she is a lady of status. Since both of my parents were doctors and I came from a wealthy family, she tried in the past to get Brandon and me to date. But Brandon is like the brother I never had. He has never said anything inappropriate to me.

You have nothing to be intimidated about. Brandon loves you and always will."

"Thank you. It's good hearing this from you. I see you have Brandon's best interest at heart. When we have our meeting I promise to back you all the way. I too would like to see him well and back to practicing medicine again."

Olivia got out of her seat and came over and gave me a big hug. I held her tight as the tears started to flow down my face. I said to myself, "Thank you, God."

Chapter Thirty Six

I spent most of the night tossing and turning. My thoughts were on how was Brandon going to take Olivia's suggestion about being his kidney donor. I finally got up to have a warm glass of milk. When I got near the kitchen I saw the light on. I walked in and there was Olivia sitting at the counter with a cup in the front of her.

"Can't sleep?"

"No. I was just thinking on how Brandon was going to take your suggestion. Would he think about his career or think about yours? His sister and I wanted to be tissue tested, but he refused our offer. How are you going to get him to change his mind?"

"Linda, all I know is that I have been fasting and praying on this. I just didn't wake up and decide to come here and be a donor. I've been talking with God about this and I feel like He is the one who will give me the words to say when I speak with Brandon. I also feel like He is the one who will soften Brandon's heart to accept my offer."

"Okay, on that note, I'm going to drink this hot milk and go back to bed, but this time I'm going to sleep."

"Goodnight. See you in the morning."

I was sleeping hard, when I heard Brianna crying. I jumped up and looked next to me. Brandon was already out of the bed. I put on my robe and house slippers and headed for the nursery. When I got there Brandon was already picking up Brianna and talking to her. I just stood there looking at them together. I was happy to see him feeling stronger this morning. Then sadness crossed my face, because tomorrow would be Wednesday, and he would have to take another treatment. Those treatments wipe him out for a day.

I walked in and swung my arms around him and Brianna. He leaned down and kissed me on the forehead. I told him I would take care of her. He said that he would get freshened up for the day.

After getting Brianna and myself dressed, I went to the kitchen to start breakfast. Olivia was sitting at the counter reading her Bible and drinking a cup of flavored coffee.

"Good morning, Linda."

"Good morning, Olivia."

Brandon walked in saying good morning to both of us. He said since there wasn't anything on the stove, why don't we go out for breakfast. Olivia said she felt like eating some pancakes with sausages. I said I wanted some Bob Evans buttermilk pancakes and bacon. We got ready and before we knew it, we all were in the car and on our way to Bob Evans for breakfast.

After breakfast Brandon took us sight-seeing. Olivia and I both enjoyed the ride. When we finally made it back home, Brianna was ready for a nap. After getting her situated, I told Olivia this was a good time to talk with Brandon. She said she wanted to go to her room for prayer. I told her to just meet us in the family room when she was ready.

When I walked into the family room, Brandon was already sitting and looking at the sports channel. I wanted to know who was playing and who was winning. I was really just making conversation because I would have been watching a movie.

Olivia came in and sat in the chair across from us. She asked Brandon if he minded turning off the TV. She told him that she had something important to talk about. Brandon took the remote control and shut the TV off.

Olivia said, "Brandon you have always been like the brother I never had. We have gone through a lot together. You were there for me when my parents were killed and I feel like you will be there for me from now on."

"Olivia, what's this all about?"

"Brandon, please let me do the talking. You just listen. I'm so sorry for your health failing you. I do want you to know that I thank you for letting me go with you to your treatment. However, it burdens me to see how weak you were after the treatment. You're a great physician and it hurts me to see that you are unable to practice medicine at this time. I have a suggestion for you. I have been tissue typed and I think my kidney would be a match for you."

Brandon stood up and said, "Olivia, thank you for the offer, but I can't let you do this. What if you do and decide one day to get married and have children. What if you had an accident and the one kidney was punctured. Then you would have to go on dialysis and not be able to be a doctor or a full-time mother."

"Brandon, please sit down. I have prayed and prayed

before coming here. When my parents died, I made up my mind that I was going to open an innercity clinic and take care of people with no insurance. I have a different outlook on life. It's not about how much money you have, it's about what can you do to help your fellow man while you are here on earth. I believe that my purpose in life is to care for the poor. Now, you said what if I fall and puncture my only kidney? Then I'll have to go on dialysis. I feel in my heart that I am being led by the Holy Spirit to give you one of my kidneys. By being obedient, God is going to protect me and not let anything happen to me. I just ask you to please let me do this for you."

Brandon was sitting there with tears welling up in his eyes. He dropped his head and said a faint "Yes. I miss caring for the sick. Yes, please help me." He then fell down on his knees and raised both hands towards heaven and said, "Lord, please let her kidney be a match. I'll serve you for the rest of my life!"

I knelt down with him and held him in my arms. We both started praying for God to show us a miracle. When we got off our knees Olivia was sitting there softly praying. I went over and held her in my arms. We both started crying and thanking God at the same time.

We called Brandon's parents to tell them that Olivia was going to be a donor for Brandon. They were happy and said they would be here when the surgery was scheduled.

* *

Praise the Lord! The operations went well and both Brandon and Olivia were recovering nicely. However, just three days after his surgery, his body began to attack the donor organ and the symptoms of his disease returned. Dr. Hammond started aggressive blood transfusion therapy. The therapy worked, so the body started to accept the kidney. Olivia was discharged in a week, but she wanted to stay around until she knew for a fact that Brandon was out of danger. It was a long two weeks, but I enjoyed having her in my home.

While I was waiting for Brandon to be released, I remembered the conversation Olivia and Brandon had a few weeks ago. Brandon asked her if she would consider moving to Georgia, in a year or two to open a clinic for the poor. She promised him she would think about it.

When the nurse wheeled Brandon to the pick up area, he had a big smile on his face. We were all smiling: Lynda, Carlos, Mother Liz, Daddy Alexander, Olivia, and my parents. He was so happy to see all of us, and more importantly, happy to have his life back.

Brandon stood and thanked the nurse. He said, "I first would like to thank God for taking me through the storms and the rain. I thank my wife for being with me during this ordeal. I thank you Olivia for giving me one of your kidneys and most of all I thank my family for your love and support. Now let's have a group hug and get me home to my daughter and a home-cooked meal."

About The Author

Francine A. Yates lives in Indianapolis, Indiana with her two adult children Donald and Patrice.

She attended Indiana University/Purdue University in Indianapolis.

Fran has been a mentor at several Indianapolis Public Schools.

She created a book club at the Wheeler Unit Boys & Girls Club of Indianapolis.

Fran's active membership includes: Pleasant Union Missionary Baptist Church, and Church Women United.

Fran's work has been published in the *Indianapolis Star*, and in 2003 she founded Yates Publishing, LLC

To schedule Book Signings or Speaking Engagements:

Francine A. Yates
P.O. Box 18982
Indianapolis, Indiana 46218
Fran3214@yahoo.com
www.franyates.net

Order Form

Name: _____

Address: _____

City: _____ State _____ Zip Code _____

_____ # of Copies of **Through the Storms and the Rain** $13.00

_____ # of Copies for **Faith Holds the Key** $14.95

_____ # of Copies of **Carrie O and Me** $14.95

_____ # of Copies of **Strength for the Journey** $12.00

INDIANA RESIDENTS ONLY and 7% sale tax:

    Shipping & Handling $3.00 _____

    Additional Shipping & Handling Cost _____
      (Add a $1.00 for each additional book)

    Total Amount Due $ _____

Mail Payment to:
Yates Publishing, LLC
P.O. Box 18982
Indianapolis, IN 46218

www.ingramcontent.com/pod-product-compliance
Lightning Source LLC
Chambersburg PA
CBHW071852220626
47052CB00002B/82

9 780977 852130